Don't Pet the Sharks

Advice, Observations &
Snark from the Big Island, Hawaii

By
Kona Lowell

authorHOUSE®

AuthorHouse™
1663 Liberty Drive, Suite 200
Bloomington, IN 47403
www.authorhouse.com
Phone: 1-800-839-8640

First published by AuthorHouse 2/11/2010

ISBN: 978-1-4490-6435-8 (e)
ISBN: 978-1-4490-6433-4 (sc)
ISBN: 978-1-4490-6434-1 (hc)

Library of Congress Control Number: 2010900461

Printed in the United States of America
Bloomington, Indiana

This book is printed on acid-free paper.

Cover illustration by Judith Johnson
Back cover photo by Brian C. Davis

TABLE OF CONTENTS

To

Kiko, Biscuit, Moku, Ipo, Katie, Okee, The Beeker and Baby Miu
for their unconditional love
and to Chee
for coming as close as is humanly possible.

A Note from the Author

The following stories, poems, rants and observations were written over the past several years and were compiled just as written. I mention this because a few of the situations have changed (we now have a Saturday newspaper, for example), some people in them have died and yet others have moved on to positions less likely to allow them to launch immediate Armageddon. I suppose I could have edited these pieces to make them more current, but I felt that the original should remain unchanged, if for no other reason than to serve as an obscure historical footnote. And I'm lazy. And my mind wanders. Which is why these pieces are usually short.

But EDSD (Extreme Debilitating Sluglike Disorder) is not the only reason it took me so long to come out with the long-awaited (dreaded?) follow-up to the groundbreaking *The Solid Green Birthday and Other Fables.* As my muse would have it, I got caught up in one of the two other things I really, really enjoy, which is playing music, and so spent about a year in the studio putting out the CD *Empire* with my band No Empty Sky. It is really wonderful. You should buy several copies (www.noemptysky.com) just in case I ever get famous. It could happen.

I was also delayed for several months trying to come up with a cover design. As you will know, if you read *TSGBAOF* (dontcha just love acronyms?), I used to be a graphics designer. The words "used to" are operative here. It means I suck at it. So after many false starts, I implored my sister, Judith Johnson, to apply her wealth of artistic sensibility to the problem.

The result is the fabulous cover art she created that graces this little book and makes it appear more significant than it really is. Imagine the danger we would all face if she was into commercial art. She could sell us anything. Thanks, Judith!

I should also mention that a couple of these pieces appeared on the CounterPunch website a few years ago, so that déjà vu you may be feeling is nothing to worry about. That déjà vu you may be feeling is nothing to worry about.

Another piece, *Hawaii Dos and Don'ts*, was the inspiration for a Learning Channel special of the same name. You can see me in the very beginning of the show, mouthing the remaining 30 seconds of my 3 minute monologue that didn't get edited out. Sometimes it gets me a free drink.

Anyway, it is my sincere hope that you will find this an amusing read. I will begin immediately working on the next book just in case and should have it completed in 6 or 7 years.

Wow. That was exhausting. Time for a nap.

ADVENT

Look out world.

Here I come,

a flaming jack-o-lantern tumbling down

the front porch steps onto the dead October lawn.

All smiles.

Look out world.

Here I come,

a wounded bomber,

trailing clouds

of dense black industry,

part-time jobs and retirement communities.

On fire.

Look out world.

Here I come,

a glacier of meth,

scraping the moss off your stones,

dredging up the long ago for here and now.

Run, run.

Look out world.

Here I come,

the song of a sword,
whistling through blood and bone,
canceling the new fall lineup.
Time's up.

Here I come.
Ready or not.
Here I come.

It's good to be home.

Don't Pet the Sharks

One thing most people notice almost as soon as they arrive in Hawaii is that they are on an island surrounded by a lot of water. In fact, you can see the ocean just about everywhere you go, unless you close your eyes. Because of this, and our boringly pleasant weather, people tend to get in this water and swim around. We call this "having fun" and do it ourselves, even those of us who live here year in and year out. But to make it safer for you tourists, allow me to give you some advice.

It is important to remember that the ocean is *not* a lake. Lakes have bass in them. Sometimes these are big bass. They like shiny things. They eat shiny minnows. We have fish that are bigger than bass. They are everywhere. They eat sea turtles and seals. To break up the monotony, they occasionally sample people. We call them "sharks."

This is not intended to scare you. Shark attacks are very rare. But that will not be much comfort to remember if one is swimming off with your leg, so here are some tips to keep you safe in our friendly, shark-filled waters.

1. Always swim with a partner. This is called the "Buddy System." It improves your chances of survival by 50% in a shark attack, unless there are two sharks.

2. When a shark attacks, punch it in the nose as hard as you can. I got this tip from an older, experienced one-armed diver named Lefty.

3. Even though they are considered chic, avoid wearing an all-meat bathing suit, except at the pool and for casual shopping.

4. Don't pet the sharks, even if they seem to be asleep. Apply that old adage about letting sleeping dogs lie. Then multiply it by 1,000.

5. Turtle and seal costumes should be worn in the ocean only on Halloween by very, very depressed people.

6. When spear fishing, resist the temptation to make a lei out of your catch until you exit the water.

7. Sharks, though intelligent, have no concept of the words "sit," "stay" or "let go."

8. Avoid swimming at "feeding time," which is approximately at dawn and dusk, unless you have a burning desire to be part of the "food chain." Yes, sharks do eat at other times of the day. They are noted snackers.

9. Avoid wearing shiny jewelry when swimming. See comment on bass fishing above.

10. When swimming with friends, avoid using the "wounded dolphin call" to keep track of each other.

11. Do not go shark fishing on any boat called the *Orca*.

12. Sharks have a limited, some might even say primeval, sense of humor. When joking your way out of an encounter, keep it simple and avoid elaborate puns.

13. Before going in the ocean, check for any gaping wounds or excessive bleeding. Apply a tourniquet.

14. Small children should be tied together on a rope at ten foot intervals. Attach a large glass sea-fishing bobber to either end.

15. Study shark behavior. This way when a shark arches its back and wags its tail, you will not confuse it with your dog Fluffy's similar body language.

16. On a crowded beach, always chum the end furthest from where you're swimming.

17. Should the unthinkable happen, remember that only a thumb and pinkie are required to make the "shaka" or "howzit" sign, our state's folksy "hello" hand gesture.

I hope this has been of some help. Remember, your chances of being attacked by one of our playful sharks is less than being struck by lightning.*

* Note: Mr Don Frick of Hamlin, PA, since you have been struck not once but twice by lightning, it is highly recommended you stay on the beach.

CELEBRITY

When does celebrity become a burden and anonymity become the goal? To discover the answer to this weighty conundrum I set out to find some famous people and learn for myself.

"Hello! Rick Jameson, right?"

"Yes?"

"I'm doing some research on fame and would like to ask you a question."

"Okay. Shoot."

"When does celebrity become a burden and anonymity become the goal?"

"I don't get it."

"When does *celebrity* become a burden and *anonymity* become the goal?"

"No, I heard you the first time. I just don't get it. What do you mean?"

"Well, your brother caught the second largest marlin in the National Billfish Tournament in '91, right"

"Yeah."

"Well, that must be an awesome responsibility to have to carry that around."

"Huh?"

"I mean the pressure to repeat must be enormous. You probably were inundated with requests to meet your brother, to see pictures of the fish, to ride on other people's boats. It must have been a terrible burden, and I would imagine there were times when you wished you could go back to your old life before you were famous."

"Not really. It wasn't that big a deal."

"Then I gather you are one of those rare individuals who is quite comfortable, or we might even say 'at home' with fame."

"Yeah, I guess. I never really thought about it. It wasn't a big deal."

"So since '91, how many second place marlins has your brother landed?"

"I really don't know."

"You don't know, or are you simply trying to avoid the spotlight?"

"No, I really don't know."

"Maybe the fame *has* become a bit of a burden?"

"Yeah, okay, maybe. I don't know."

"Then will you be changing your Yellow Pages ad? The one that says *Go fishing with Rick Jameson, brother of the guy who caught the second largest marlin in the 1991 International Billfish Tournament.*"

"Well, maybe. I don't know. Hey, I've really gotta go, man."

"Okay, but can I see the picture of that marlin first?"

"Yeah, sure. Here it is."

"Wow. That's some fish."

"Yeah. Hey look, I've gotta go, man."

"Getting to be a bit of a burden, is it not, my friend? I understand."

Those of us who have not experienced what it is like to be a celebrity can only imagine the awesome weight these people must bear every day of their lives. Maybe if we realized the overwhelming, crushing burden they carry, a burden that rests like the world on Atlas' mighty, aching back, we would be more forgiving of their human frailties: their womanizing, public drunkenness, drug convictions, shoplifting and pederasty.

And maybe, knowing of this backbreaking responsibility, we will be less inclined to wish for fame ourselves, to wish we had brothers who caught second place marlins, and got free beer and girls who like fishermen. It is not all parties and riding parade floats and full answering machines.

Just ask Rick Jameson.

THE VERY PRAYING MAN

I met a very praying man on the roadside. His eyes and arms were raised to heaven, his mouth a blur. His knees were deep in mud, the soles of his shoeless feet blackened with the grime of traffic.

"For what do you pray, pilgrim bold?" I queried.

He turned his fervent gaze on me, and replied with due solemnity, "A ride to town, my friend, is all I seek. But the Good Lord seems unwilling to hear my heartsick pleas. I have been praying here for lo this many hours, till my knees are numb and my lips chapped, but not a single car has altered its course to rescue me from my long distress. I fear that God has become deaf to my solicitations and no more cares for my sorrows and afflictions."

"Maybe if you got out of this 8 foot deep ditch and stood up next to the road where people could actually *see* you, someone might stop and give you a ride," I suggested.

"Ah, my friend, God needs not the "easy way," he said, making vigorous air quotes with his fingers. "He sees me quite clearly down here."

"True," I answered, "but I don't think God is going to drive by. It wouldn't be cheating to at least stand up, would it?"

"I shall not limit my God, my friend. I shall not limit my God."

With that I continued my journey along the ditch, filling the rest of my sack with discarded cans and plastic bottles. Suddenly there was a deafening roar as of a whirlwind and blowing dust filled the air. I threw myself on the ground, covering my ears and looked skyward to see a golden chariot pass quickly overhead. Out the right hand side the very praying man was waving to me and smiling.

Well, so much for parables I thought to myself.

PERFECT

If I could change anything
it would be my nose

and maybe my legs
and the shape of my head

and my hair

and my voice

and my eyebrows

and my front teeth

bigger muscles

but other than that
I'm pretty happy with myself.

ONE WONDERFUL WEEK

I guess I should really be ashamed of myself, and I am, but I had a wonderful week. Sure, I get good days now and then. I can remember one in June of 1987, but seven days in a row is sort of miraculous.

The reason I say I should be ashamed is that this whole week of happiness came as a result of my girlfriend being sick. Nothing serious, just got a bad cold, which she quickly recovered from. It was the laryngitis that turned out to be something really special.

This was the first time since I have known her that she was entirely unable to speak. I don't mean she was hoarse, I mean she could not make a sound, beyond an almost inaudible squeak, like an anemic mouse with emphysema. It was wonderful.

I said I was ashamed already, okay?

This changed everything. First of all, we could not talk on the phone. We were forced to use Yahoo Messenger and chat back and forth on our computers, and since I type a blazing 20 words per minute (with typos), this made for short conversations. In other words, we got to the meat right away. It was incredible.

"I go store way home."

"OK."

"MNF at 7, Vikes v. Skins. Pizza."

"OK."

No, I'm the one saying "OK." She really loves football.

And guess what was the one thing we couldn't do? That's right: argue. Now you're seeing my point, huh?

At home, it was even less wordy, since she had to write on one of those erasable refrigerator grocery list things. This kept our conversation to single words for the most part. Like cavemen with Sharpies.

It was tough, but I fought the overpowering urge to come home every night and say, "Well, tell me all about your day!"

But all good things come to an end, and after a week, her voice began to return. I had gone through a whole seven days without once hearing, "You never listen to anything I say."

I have heard that several times since then, but I don't mind. She had a lot of stored up words and plenty to say after being mute for a week. So I am working on being a good listener. And I must admit that "I love you" has more impact when it's spoken than when it's written on one of those refrigerator things in purple.

Still, it was a wonderful week. It might be good for our relationship to have a wordless vacation like this every few years, but unfortunately I can't count on her getting laryngitis again.

So I'm taking up scuba. Did you know that you can go deaf for days if you don't clear your ears properly when diving?

Hawaiian Language Can Make You Go Completely Insane

Wouldn't think a language with only 12 letters could do that, would you? Bwaaa haaa haaa haaa!

The thing is, Hawaiians enjoy stringing word after word together to make new words, which allows them to use these same twelve letters (a, e, i, o, u, p, k, h, l, m, n, w and the glottal stop, or *'okina*) over and over. It makes for a very complex, poetic and fascinating language and an innocent means of embarrassing the hell out of *haole* tourists, while still being charming. Here's a common example, the name of our cute little state fish: *humuhumunuknukuapua'a*.

Now if you live here, you most likely have no problem repeating that (when sober). You also probably know that it means "trigger fish (*humuhumu*) with a nose (*nukunuku*) like a pig (*a pua'a*)." Or you might remember the song *My Little Grass Shack in Kealakekua, Hawaii* which contains the line "Where the *humuhumunukunukuapua`a* go swimming by," a song we all sing daily here while pounding poi, stringing leis, surfing, perfecting our tans and weaving *lau hala* hats and making plans to secede from the Union.

Fortunately, most tourists can avoid saying *humhumunukunukuapua'a* as it rarely comes up in conversation, but they can't avoid trying to pronounce our mind-boggling place names because they are trying to get to those places.

Take a simple one like Keauhou, located about midway between Kailua-Kona and Kealakekua. It's got some serious vowel action going on. Five vowels, two consonants. Or the famous Place of Refuge, Pu'uhonua o Honaunau. Or a hot spot you're likely to visit if you come to the Big Island, Kilauea, our famous volcano (while there, be sure to check out the Pu'u O'o cone and Halemaumau crater).

Seems a bit daunting, no? But do not get discouraged. Did you take Spanish in high school? Okay. Pronounce all the vowels the same way. The consonants you already know how to pronounce, except that the "w" can be a bit tricky. Sometimes it sounds like a "v", sometimes like a "w". Fake it. But here's the important thing: pronounce *every* vowel. If you do that, you will at least get close enough to be understood.

Now try "Keauhou." Kay-ah-oo-HO-oo. Now run it all together really fast and you've got it. Can of corn. And not as laughable as Kee-ah-HOO. Well, actually it is, but one is correct and the other isn't.

Anyway, you'll eventually get the hang of it, or you'll just give up and point at things on a map. Either way you'll probably get where you're going.

Unless someone gives you directions in pidgin.

Heaven

Heaven always sounded like a good idea to me. I used to want to go there someday, hopefully at the last possible minute. But now I'm not so sure.

See, I have a very short attention span, which is why I can't watch miniseries on TV or go to the opera. I can't read anything by Michener or Tolstoy. I don't play chess. I write short, stupid stories. I can't even stay interested in the same girl for too long, unless she has a sister maybe.

Heaven goes on forever.

I keep wondering what I would do there for eternity. Eternity is kinda scary if you have a very short attention span.

Sure, it would be really great to see God. I bet I would be amazed and thrilled. But I'm thinking that after a billion or so years the novelty might start to wear off.

Of course since I've never been to heaven I really don't know if it would be boring. Maybe they don't have any clocks up there so you don't realize you've been staring at God for a billion years. And maybe they have activities, like Club Med. And an open bar.

There's also the obvious downside of spending eternity with people you never liked too much. It's bad enough when you have to see them once in a while, like at a class reunion, and be nice to them. You can always leave. I don't think you can leave heaven.

Then there's all those people who are supposed to be there that I *really* don't like. It would be my kinda luck to end up rooming with Pat Robertson and Jerry Falwell. For *ever*.

Please let there be an open bar.

LYCHEE

She loves eating lychee
fresh off the tree
here in Hawaii

It brings back her childhood
in Hong Kong
the good times

she spits out the seeds

the bad times.

MAYANS

My friend Alexis is a poet, which makes her of course entirely unreliable where reality or even everyday life is concerned. Still, she makes me think, which can be a good thing as long as you don't overdo it.

The other day she wrote to rattle my brain with two highly imaginative and interesting concepts. One, that her cat, Oscar, is really an alien, and two, that the Mayans built all those tall buildings and pyramids just so they could see over the jungle.

I should say right here that Alexis is not insane, but as I mentioned earlier, a poet, so she thinks like this. And these radical assumptions are not based on mere whims, but on careful observation.

For example, she arrived at this theory about Oscar being an alien by observing his highly unusual behavior. He sits like a meerkat, or a prairie dog, on his haunches, and stares around. He does this at the foot of her bed, staring at her, so this is what she sees when she first wakes up. Sorta creepy.

I would hasten to agree that this is distinctly alien behavior, except that my cat does the exact same thing.

I always assumed that my jellicle cat, Kiko, picked this weirdness up from our mongoose, who sits like that all the time. But now, since Oscar, miles away and not under any mongoose influence whatsoever does the same thing, I must admit Alexis' original hypothesis.

Cats are aliens.

This leads me to the inevitable conclusion that the Mayans were aliens. Or cats.

This is obvious from their culture which deified the jaguar and their artwork which portrayed people with fierce jaguar features, producing very odd looking human beings. It is clear that this is *exactly* the kind of human a cat would appreciate: someone with a hideous jaguar face.

But this doesn't explain all the tall pyramidal buildings rising out of the Yucatan jungles. Or *does* it?

Everybody knows that cats like heights. They like to get up on the tallest thing they can find. These pyramids are just gigantic cat playhouses. They could go up on top of these pyramids and sit on their haunches and watch the birds, and other cats, sitting on *their* haunches, across the jungle. Even the names of these places are catlike. Take Chichen Itza for example. Sounds like some kind of cat food. Coincidence? I don't think so.

The sudden disappearance of the Mayans has always been one of the greatest of archaeological mysteries. Theories have abounded for years, debates have raged, arriving at no general consensus. But the Mayans did *not* disappear. They were assimilated. Not into the Mesoamerican societies that surrounded them, but into ours. Do not look for them in the swarthy, adventurous Latin or the colorful Indians still inhabiting the region, but in the purring jaguar-like creature in your lap.

A wild fantasy? The ravings of an archaeological anarchist? The mental drooling of a historically challenged imbecile? Maybe. Or is it just coincidence that the word "Maya" is a bald-faced corruption of "meow"? Chichen Itza for thought, my friend, Chichen Itza for thought.

Mr. Fixit

Some people are born with mechanical aptitude, like my dad, a professional engineer. He can build anything or fix anything. He's a wiz. When I was a kid, he built our TV, our stereo, even our furniture. He had a lathe in the garage for making his own machine parts, so he could make his own machines. None of this ever rubbed off on me.

As a child, I was more interested in cooking.

When I got a bit older, making model cars was a big craze. On rainy Saturdays my friends would huddle in their garages, assembling their '57 Chevys, delicately painting each part and painstakingly adding funny fur to the upholstery. I used to just hit the whole thing with a can of spray paint so I could get to the fun part — sticking the decals on. Then I would go work on a new bouillabaisse recipe.

When I got older still, driving age, my friends would have these intense debates about hemis and Hurst shifters and headers and all sorts of other things that I believe had to do with cars. They loved this stuff. Their fingernails were black. None of it made any sense to me, so I bought a motorcycle. I used to repair it by beating it with a hammer. Eventually I bought a '65 Beetle. I beat it with a hammer, too.

I am not proud of this. It is good for a man to be able to fix things. It gets you dinner and sex. I was never that concerned about the dinner part, because by then I was a pretty good cook. So I learned to play music, which worked just about as well on the sex thing.

Still, there is something in me that wants to be handy. One time my girlfriend had a leaky toilet. I figured this couldn't be too difficult to deal with. I'd seen plumbers before and they never struck me as magical, or even particularly bright. Not only that, they never even seemed to realize that their butt cracks were showing when they had their heads under the sink. Even I am more aware than that. So I got a wrench and went to work. Here's a tip: always know where the water main is *before* you pull a pipe out of the wall.

This did not stop me, unfortunately. I still possessed this need to be helpful. One day I saw two beautiful women stranded with a flat tire. Even I had changed tires before. Sure, it took me several tries, busted a knuckle or two, but I had done it. I could do it again. I approached the desperate women and gallantly offered my services. They were thrilled and cooing encouragement. I tried to imagine myself in the pits at Indy, while keeping up a confident, manly banter.

"Yeah, as soon as I get this tire on, I'll treat you both to a drink."

"That would be wonderful," they purred. Thank you God.

Unfortunately, they had one of those new jacks that I had never seen before, and putting it on upside down, I broke it. I was forced to go call a mechanic, which I did really, really well. I think he took them out for drinks.

Today I know my limitations. I occasionally hang a picture, change a light bulb or pour Drano down the sink. I have a small, very unprofessional-looking toolbox with a screwdriver, pliers, a saw and a good strong hammer for car repairs.

My Nudist Life

I am a confirmed nudist. Most people don't realize this, but it's true. That's because every time they see me I have clothes on. But underneath that t-shirt and jeans I'm gloriously — profoundly — naked.

Knowing this, it did take me some time to get comfortable with the idea. I used to blush when I went into the grocery store, knowing how naked I really was. I was just glad I had a shopping cart in front of me. And meeting people for the first time always brought out my shyness. Were they uneasy with my nakedness? Were they desperately trying to look me in the eyes? Were they sneaking peeks when I wasn't looking?

It took a while, but now I'm pretty much okay with my nudist life. I can go to the grocery store and just use one of those little baskets instead of a cart. I can meet new people and not worry that they're checking me out. I don't care a bit that they know how naked I am under these clothes. It is a terrific feeling of freedom. It's the way we were meant to be. It's natural.

But I still can't play volleyball.

Shopping

I have enough angst, thank you

but I could use some more

foreboding

and a case of the heebie-jeebies,

caffeine–free

please

The Iron Clown Triathlon

A couple days ago while having brunch at my friend Nick's house, I watched an amazing race on the tube, the Xterra Maui. I had never heard of this competition, but am familiar with triathlons since we have the Ironman here on the Big Island every year. This was different.

The Xterra, sponsored by Nissan, is an off-road race, comprised of a 1.5km ocean swim, a 30km mountain bike race and an 11km trail run. The Maui course was especially brutal, with the biking taking place on steep, rocky trails as well as knee-deep dirt and the run traversing *kiawe* forests, beach sand and sharp, pointy rocks. The competitors were forced to follow trails that dove under tree branches and over fallen logs. Most of the contestants, even those that finished, were bruised and bloodied at the tape. How many did not finish or were carted off I can only imagine.

Which made me think this would make an excellent sport for clowns.

As you may know, if you have read *The Solid Green Birthday and Other Fables*, I am not a fan of clowns (I Hate Clowns, p. 21). So the thought of this race possibly eliminating some of them is the sort of concept I'd love to see realized. Immediately.

Nothing need be changed, except that instead of top world athletes vying for the title, the field would be restricted to clowns only. And instead of wearing bike shorts and bathing suits, they would have to compete in their clown regalia. There would of course be regular divisions for sex and age, if possible to determine.

Now in the first part of the race, the 1.5km swim, the clowns with the biggest shoes would have an obvious edge. These grotesque pedal extremity accessories are very similar to scuba fins or flippers and will propel the clown through the water at a high rate of speed. Or they would, if they were not wearing the rest of their hideous costumes. It is possibly that due to the bagginess of the clothing, the field of contestants will be depleted considerably in the first part of the race. Those that wear the pants that have that hoop sort of thing that makes them stand out from the waist will experience severe problems, as this will act as an underwater parachute, rendering them virtually immobile, and I should expect, easy pickings for our always hungry water creatures. Note: Remind all clowns to use waterproof makeup. Shark repellant is not allowed.

Those who survive the swim will next proceed to the 30km mountain bike course. There will be a small change in this part, as the clowns will not be riding mountain bikes, but unicycles. They may, however, be fitted with a mountain bike tire. And as in the regular Xterra, the clown may carry or push his/her/its unicycle up and down the trails as necessary. They will, however, be followed closely at all times by a very aggressive and foul-tempered monkey, dressed like a perverse, deranged bellhop, on a small motorcycle to insure that there is no cheating and who will attack them viciously if they fall down. Hitting other clowns with pies or squirting them in the face with seltzer will *not* be considered cheating at any time during the race.

Now it's on to the 11km trail run for those few lucky enough to make it that far. Like the regular Xterra run, it will take the hardy, and by now bloody, bedraggled and aching clowns through deep, tangled forests, sandy beaches and dangerously rocky shorelines. There will only be a few subtle changes: wild boars (released at race time) and a handful of tiger pits, hidden here and there along the trail.

The first place winners in all age and sex divisions will receive $5,000 dollars each and tickets and plane fare to The International Clown Hall of Fame in West Allis, Wisconsin. From there they will be flown, one-way, to France.

I know some people will consider this idea extravagant, what with the billions we're spending fighting terrorism and all, but the few hundred thousand this would cost to rid the world of clowns would be of lasting benefit to mankind. Think of the children. The Department of Homeland Security probably has a few extra bucks lying around. Somewhere. Besides, it would be really fun to watch. In slow motion.

Who knows, if this catches on, there could be all sorts of thrilling spin-offs. The Xterra Senate Race would be huge.

Jesus' Really Lousy Bio

I hate to say it, but I have a problem with the Bible, and it's not what you think it is. Sure, the Old Testament is full of out-dated food pyramids and politically incorrect social dictates, a mind-numbing list of rules and regulations about virtually every aspect of life and personal hygiene, as well as more senseless violence than the average Schwarzenegger film inflicts, but my problem lies elsewhere. It's in the New Testament.

What bothers me is the writing, specifically that of four men: Matthew, Mark, Luke and John. You know, the guys who wrote what we call the Gospels, and after which half of the boys born during the '50s were named. They were lousy writers. Sorry.

Now don't get me wrong. I am not finding fault with their beliefs, only their awful way of expressing those beliefs. Let me explain.

Here you have four guys who are pretty much insiders writing about arguably the most important man to ever walk the planet. Not only do they plagiarize each other constantly, they seem to be unable to find much to say. Just look at how thick one gospel is compared to, say, Deuteronomy. It's like a chapter!

Now I realize that this was written a couple thousand years ago and the idea of the "novel" hadn't been conceived yet, but come on, guys, how about a bit of background? Description? Humor? Pacing?

Ever wonder what Jesus might have looked like? I do. I can almost guarantee he didn't look anything like Peter O'Toole or Jeffrey Hunter or Willem Dafoe, none of which are Semites, as far as I can tell. Or maybe what he did for the first 30 years of his life? I mean aside from a little blip about him worrying his parents silly by ditching the caravan and hanging out at the temple to confound to the rabbis, we know virtually nothing.

Did the other kids in the neighborhood, or his dozen or so brothers and sisters, know he was the Messiah? Did they razz him about it or what? More importantly, did *he* know? This would only be a hundred times worse than being Clark Kent.

And how about Mary? Did mom play favorites like most do? Surely she knew he was special, but then what mom doesn't think her first born is? And what happened to his dad, Joseph? He just disappears after a really brief cameo. No explanation, no goodbyes, nada. Got less face time than Trini Lopez in The Dirty Dozen.

This is especially irritating when you realize how many biographies there are about people who really don't deserve them or already have several. Just go to Amazon and take a look. I went to Biographies and Memoirs, People A to Z. I then went to the J section. There were the expected Thomas Jefferson and Andrew Jackson bios. But I didn't expect a couple dozen of these. Then there were also the Michael Jackson and Michael Jordan bios. But, nope, not a single Jesus. And the guys that could have written this incredible biography were content to simply assemble some quotes, jot down a few miracles and call it a day. Slackers.

Matthew writes in his 5th chapter:

And seeing the multitudes, he went up into a mountain: and when he was set, his disciples came unto him: And he opened his mouth, and taught them, saying, "Blessed are the poor in spirit: for theirs is the kingdom of heaven."

But what if Matt had written it like this:

Jesus was exhausted. It was hot today, even for Palestine and this rocky region had only scrub brush and a few gnarled and disfigured trees. There was no shade. The sweat poured down his dark, aquiline face as he surveyed the needy, anxious crowd that had followed him from place to place for the last several days. He needed a break, and some sleep, but with a resigned sigh, he began to climb the mountain at whose crumbling feet the multitude had assembled. When he reached a large, flat boulder, he sat down and waited for his tired, grumbling disciples to catch up. Fortunately for him, years of carpentry had kept him in good shape and he still enjoyed a long run on the beach — when he could escape the ever-enlarging crowds.

Finally, his puffing and panting disciples reached the boulder on which their teacher sat, arms folded and smiling. Peter, also in good training, and who had tolerantly helped some of the less athletic ones up, gave Jesus a knowing look and arched his eyebrows a couple times. Jesus just smiled and shook his head. Tax collectors don't get a lot of exercise, except when they're being chased out of town.

Jesus scanned the restless crowd below him. Every face was looking up at him, waiting. He studied the faces: old, young, worn and fresh, but all expectant. A sudden memory startled him, as he remembered sitting on Joseph's knee and thrilling to tales of lions and warriors and kings of old. He took a gulp of water from his nearly empty skin and cleared his throat.

"Blessed are the poor in spirit, for theirs is the kingdom of heaven…"

Okay, not very good perhaps, but you get the point. This could have been interesting, not just enlightening. They could have fleshed Jesus out, made him seem human, which he was, instead of just some humorless, stern guru mouthing platitudes. This was a man from a podunk town, who worked with his hands, had a family, ate food and even went to the bathroom (or whatever they called it back then). He got tired, knew sadness and joy, pain and pleasure. I wish Matthew and his fellow writers, especially John who was really close to Jesus, had seen fit to impart a bit more of this humanity to us.

We know more about Luke Skywalker.

A Bird in the Hand

Kevin was just sitting there, minding his own business after a long day, stretched out on a lawn chair in the back yard, a smoke in one hand and a beer in the other, watching the color drain from the Kona sky.

His wife and the boys were in the house and his thoughts drifted from music to work and back again. Lots to do. It'll all get done. What was the name of that song?

Suddenly, his hand was jolted, and he dropped his beer and cigarette. Looking at his hand, he was startled to find a very small bird nestled in his palm.

He sat there for a moment, wondering if this could really be happening, then hurried into the house, the tiny bird still resting in his cupped hand.

In the light, he could see a beautiful, very small green finch with bright red tail feathers. It did not appear to be injured or interested in flying away. Still amazed, he called his wife Ikumi and the boys to witness the strange event.

The little finch sat calmly, staring back at the four wondering faces looking down at him. Only Ikumi seemed distressed by the situation.

"This is not a good sign. This means you are going to die," she said.

The little finch said nothing, but snuggled further into Kevin's hand.

Kevin took the bird back outside, looked at it closely, saw nothing ominous, and watched, still marveling, as it flew from his hand into the night.

I can't recall this happening to anyone else I know. St Francis of Assisi comes to mind, but all we really have are paintings of birds perched on him. Whether he was truly as unique as Kevin is anyone's guess.

I consider Kevin fortunate, maybe even blessed. That little bird could have landed anywhere. It chose his hand. But I know Ikumi is also correct. Kevin is going to die.

Some day.

CHARLIE

Charlie puts the new toilet on the flat-bed truck and ties it down. He adjusts his iPod and goes back to work, sanding something that needs sanding. Sawdust forms little dunes around his tennis shoes as the narrator continues the audio book that drowns out the sander. Maybe it's a Harry Potter novel. Maybe it's something by Carl Sagan. It could be Al Franken.

The workshop resembles the aftermath of a particularly powerful tornado. It is difficult to navigate through the piles of wood and tools and things hanging from the ceiling that whack taller people in the forehead. But Charlie knows where everything is. "Carpenters make chips" as my dad always said. He was right.

Charlie looks a bit like Cato (no, not the Green Hornet's sidekick, the Greek statesman) or maybe the Roman Gaius Plinius Cecilius Secundus (known to his drinking buddies as Pliny the Elder) except that he wears jeans and red suspenders by day and not a toga. Charlie only wears a toga at night.

Charlie packs up a dozen lava lamps that he has secretly made for Christmas gifts. But these are not ordinary lava lamps. He has modified them, giving them beautiful koa wood bases. There is glitter in the lava. It is a beautiful light. The people who receive them will be surprised, but not that Charlie made them.

Charlie is fortunate. He shares his intentional solitude with Jean, who shares hers with Charlie. They are a team, which is the best description of a good marriage I can think of. Jean is a local of Okinawan heritage, petite and pretty and undaunted by anything in work or life, including Charlie. She's his right hand. Charlie is fortunate. Jean helps pick the avocados. She wears a helmet just in case. Good thing, too.

Charlie wears a ring. On it are the initials MIT. I think it reminds him of why he lives in Hawaii on a mountain and raises avocados and makes things out of wood and wears red suspenders.

Charlie is a nuclear physicist. He used to work on submarines. He used to be a professor. I bet his students thought he looked like Cato, or maybe Pliny the Elder.

Pliny said "True glory consists of doing what deserves to be written; in writing what deserves to be read; and in so living as to make the world happier for our living in it."

Pliny would like Charlie. He would like Charlie's toga. They would open a bottle of cabernet and talk about avocados and wood and physics.

Pliny would say, "*In vino veritas.*"

Charlie would agree, clink glasses, and turn the hot tub up a notch.

RATS

If I were a rat
I would try to use a bit more sense.
I would enjoy the avocados
since I live in an avocado orchard.
No one will miss a few of these.

I would supplement my diet with mangoes
and papayas
and bananas
and passion fruit
and all the seeds that I could find.

And the occasional edible trash.
French fries would be nice.

I would keep an eye out for owls
and cats
and live in a safe warm place.

I would teach this to my children.

I would encourage other rats to do this
and not to make nests in nice peoples' attics
and eat their artificial Christmas trees
for God's sake.

I Want a Purse

Okay, damn it, I admit it. I want a purse. No, not something girlie-looking and stylish, just a nice leather bag I can carry over my shoulder to hold all the stuff I need. Okay? I want a Man Purse.

This is one area where we guys are screwed by our own (imagined) machismo and why we end up with bum sciatic nerves from sitting on our over-stuffed wallets. We just can't carry a purse.

Oh sure, there are a few guys that carry them, but they're mostly in New York or Europe where this is seen as trendy as opposed to really gay. Besides, they already have a high weirdness threshold there and carrying a purse could only make you seem normal, especially when the man sitting next to you on the subway is wearing a mini skirt. But try carrying one into my local bar or car repair shop or grocery store and see what happens.

See, here's the problem. I mostly wear jeans or shorts topped off with a t-shirt or tank top. I've got limited pocket space. My keys go in my left pants pocket, my wallet in my back right pocket and my smokes and lighter in my front right pocket (if my pants aren't too tight). What if I want to carry a comb? Or a book? Or a banana? Or a checkbook? Or a cell phone (I might get one. Someday). Where do I put it?

For women this is of course no problem at all. It all goes in the purse. My girlfriend's purse is so full of useful things that she could be ship-wrecked for a month with nothing but her purse and survive. Need a pen? Breath mint? Scissors? Kleenex? Needle and thread? Toenail clipper?

Rubber band? Advil? Reading glasses? Yogurt? A picture of her cat? Brass knuckles? Half a cheese sandwich? It's in there. And more.

Me? I'm carrying things around in my hands like a monkey.

Of course some men have gotten around the feminine implications of carrying a purse by the means of a very masculine briefcase. This works pretty well, unless you're wearing shorts, slippers and a tank top. For some reason, a briefcase just doesn't complete this ensemble any more than a fedora would. And you can't hang a briefcase off your barstool.

Take a look at history. No, go ahead. Men *used* to carry purses. Real men. Like trappers, and buffalo hunters and mountain men. Daniel Boone! Davy Crockett! They carried them, and some of the purses even had fringes on them. I've seen pictures. No one would have called these bearded, smelly, gun-totin' he-men sissies! You can bet that when they came down out of the mountains after months alone and into the local saloon nobody made fun of their purses. You can't be a sissy and live for months on end in a cabin in the wilderness with just some other bearded, smelly, gun-totin' bear of a man and no women and... okay, bad example.

Anyway, I still want a purse to carry all my stuff in but I don't want to be the trailblazer, thank you. I've got enough problems and I haven't forgotten all the grief I got years ago for this stupid earring. I'll just wait until someone like Stallone or Jim Belushi or Viggo Mortensen or Matthew McConaughey makes them popular and all the *real* men start carrying them. Until then I'll sit on my wallet and carry things in my hands. Like a monkey. A manly monkey.

GOD'S HURRICANE

As can be expected with any disaster, natural or man-made, the Old Testament hellfire and brimstone wing of the Evangelical junta is ready as always to explain the suffering, death and devastation as being the direct result of the usual suspects. You know, the homosexuals, liberals, Democrats, Hollywood elite, anti-war protesters and those who use reason as a means of arriving at a conclusion.

From failed prophet of doom, Hal Lindsey, to Rev. Fred Phelps (maybe one of the few people Jesus Himself would beat the living crap out of) to the ever more tragically insane Pat Robertson, all have found it easy to see Hurricane Katrina as the none too subtle instrument of God's righteous indignation at our gross and abiding sin.

Now not being of this Evangelical ilk, you may be dismayed to find that I think this triumvirate of hate may not be as wrong as we would certainly hope they are.

Maybe God *was* trying to tell us something.

Maybe He was pointing out that we Americans have rampant poverty and a generally ignored and burgeoning poor population in this the richest of all countries and that we should do something about it. Besides talk.

Maybe He was pointing out the greed, arrogance, racism and purely evil nature of this president and his oily neocon cabal. Please notice that I do not choose to list "incompetence" as one of this syndicate's faults, as I do not believe it to be a factor and also because I doubt that God would wreak biblical-style havoc just because of klutziness.

Maybe He was pointing out the very real danger of callously fiddling with Nature and the nonchalant destruction of His beautiful earth through depletion of the wetlands and global warming and careless oil exploration. He has reacted harshly to bad stewardship in the past.

Maybe He was trying to tell us there is a better place for our armed forces to be. Like in our own country. Or maybe it was His way of saying, "You think you got weapons? I got your WMD right here!"

Maybe He was trying to tell us that we really haven't overcome that race thing we think we've really overcome.

Or maybe He was just trying to tell us we are after all not as powerful and in control as we think we are. That in reality we are still just an anthill in the universe and the people of this planet like so many self-absorbed ants and that all our grand achievements can be washed away like even the very best sandcastles with one good, strong wave.

Then again, maybe it was just a bad storm and God was busy elsewhere. That is my hope, though it would be a bonus if we could get some sort of positive message out of the horror and destruction and use that new found wisdom to make this world a better place to be.

But before we do that, can we at least stone Hal Lindsey to death for being a false and very annoying prophet? It's biblical. Please?

Once Is Enough, Thanks

My friend believes in this thing called reincarnation. Don't ask me why. He just does. He never gives up on the idea that one day he'll convert me.

"Well, now I know why I like French movies so much," he informs me. "I was Napoleon in a previous life."

"You and about a million other people," I answered. "That poor guy must be getting tired of being recycled."

"No really. I remember I used to call Josephine 'Jojo'."

"Well, that proves it."

"You don't believe me?"

"No."

"Why not?"

"Well for one thing you always think you are the reincarnation of someone famous. I might believe you if you said you shoveled shit in Napoleon's *stables*, but you never do. It's always 'I was Alexander the Great or Attila the Hun or Julius Caesar or Blackbeard the Pirate.' It's never some poor, boring shoemaker or miserable eunuch with a palm fan or starving Irish potato farmer with gout."

"Can I help it if I was famous?"

Apparently he can't, nor can most of the promoters of this notion. Try to imagine Shirley McClaine bragging about a past life as a scullery maid with eleven children. Or a Chinese rice farmer with one acre of paddy. Or a Victorian Era street hooker with syphilis. Nope. Not romantic enough.

Or maybe lowly people aren't reincarnated as Hollywood stars. Maybe they've already suffered enough.

"Why do you refuse to believe me?" my friend continues, frustrated at what he sees as my bourgeois pig-headedness.

"Because it just doesn't add up," I answer. "Look, tell me this. Were Adam and Eve reincarnated?"

"No. They were the first people, if you believe such nonsense."

"Okay. But people had to start somewhere, right? So let's say Adam and Eve were not reincarnated. What about their sons, Cain and Abel. Were they reincarnated? And from whom? Adam and Eve were still alive."

"I don't know."

"So when did it start?"

"I guess when we got enough people to make it work."

"Okay. So now we have around six billion plus people on earth. According to you, they're all reincarnations of somebody else."

"Right."

"Well where did the first six billion people come from that we are now all the reincarnations of?"

"Atlantis."

Sometimes it just doesn't pay to argue. I hope my friend is wrong about reincarnation. Once is enough for me. In fact, when I talk to him, once is too many.

DIRECTIONS, BIG ISLAND STYLE

When you visit Hawaii for the first time, getting around can be a bit daunting. This isn't because we have a complicated highway system. We only have the one highway, which is mostly two lanes and goes in a big circle, at least guaranteeing you'll end up where you started from if you get lost. No, there are other reasons.

The first reason we already covered in *Hawaiian Language Can Make You Go Completely Insane*. Street names can be a real nightmare for the inexperienced. The second reason is the way we give directions.

Please understand that we're not doing this to be cruel. It's just the way it is.

Right away you will notice that there are two words that come up all the time. They are *mauka* and *makai* (MAU-kah and Mah-KAI). They mean "towards the mountain" and "towards the ocean" respectively. These will be part of any directions you get. Example:

"Can you tell me where the Hard Rock Café is?"

"Sure. The Hard Rock Café is on the *mauka* side of Ali'i Drive, next to Lulu's."

Or "Have you seen my girlfriend?"

"Sure. She's throwing up next to the seawall, just *makai* of The Hard Rock Café, next to Lulu's." (Disclaimer: This is not intended to imply that eating at the Hard Rock Café, or Lulu's, will make you throw up. I have eaten at both without hurling more than once.)

That's the easy part. Now it gets hard. Again, believe me, no one is doing this to be difficult, but many of us don't have real addresses.

This is not a problem if you are asking for directions to Sack N Save, for the most part. Someone will tell you which road to take and give you some identifiable landmark, like Burger King or Border's or something. Piece of cake.

But let's say someone invites you to his home. Unless they live at Sack N Save, not a piece of cake.

The directions will go something like this:

"Okay. Take Old Filipino Clubhouse Road."

"Where's that?"

"Where the old Filipino clubhouse used to be."

"I don't know where that is. Is there a street sign?"

"No."

So they explain where Old Filipino Clubhouse Road is by using mile markers and mailboxes and curves in the highway. So far so good.

"Now come up Old Filipino Clubhouse Road about ¼ mile until you see an old green truck. About 100 feet after that you'll come to a fork in the road. Stay left until you see a rock wall. Just past that, take the second dirt driveway and follow it around the gray house with the blue roof until you come to a cement driveway. Don't take it. Just ahead on your left you'll see a big mango tree with a tire swing. Turn in there and follow the fence. Ours is the second house with the green roof. Got it?"

What you won't know until you leave the highway, however, is that Old Filipino Clubhouse Road, like most of our rural roads, is basically a one-lane, rocky and full-of-potholes jeep trail. Always ask if 4-wheel drive is required. Ask again if they say no.

There Oughta be a Law

Normally, I am not for adding laws to the already over-burdened system we presently stagger under. There are quite a few that should have been repealed millennia ago (Did you know it's illegal to whistle in a bar in Hawaii?). But occasionally I find myself wishing certain things fell under the criminal label. Being opposed to the death penalty, I would not call for that irreversible punishment, though I must admit that a public stoning for these crimes would be enjoyably cathartic. No, I would stop short of that and only require a public (and as humiliating as possible) flogging.

Here are some worthy candidates for a really enthusiastic and painfully prolonged beating:

White people who wear dreadlocks. You know what? This only looks good on *black* people about half the time. It never looks good on white folks, unless you think cocker spaniels with mange and matted fur are attractive.

People who drive Hummers. Gee, thanks, Arnold. As if god-awful, senseless violence-filled movies weren't enough of a legacy, you give us the Neanderthalmobile. These ugly, gas-guzzling and impractical SUV's can now be seen here in rural Hawaii, driven by rich, white retirees and trust fund babies who have made this their way of giving the rest of us the finger, without having to roll down the window.

Admen who use my favorite rock 'n roll for bourgeois TV commercials. Okay, I know nothing is really sacred, but Zeppelin is *not* Cadillac music, the Godfather of Soul should not be associated with constipation and I'll kill myself if The Stones *Satisfaction* is ever used in a Viagra ad. After I kill Mick.

Sports commentators. All of them. No exceptions.

"Hey, Coach, you're down 35 points. What are you going to do in the second half?"

"Well, Mike, we're going to have to control the ball and not make any mistakes and go on down the field and score."

"Well, good luck with that plan, coach!"

Anyone who makes a film or commercial with a talking baby in it. Especially if the baby has Bruce Willis' voice. Some people find this adorable. I find it painful, in a queasy, pornographic sort of way. Use midgets instead.

The White House Press Corp (except Helen Thomas). See Sports Commentators.

People who drive with their dog in the bed of their truck, unleashed. Ever seen a dog hit the pavement going 55? I have. May have to change my mind on capital punishment for this one.

People who wait until it is pitch dark to turn their headlights on. What? Are they trying to save the battery? And have you ever noticed it's usually a dark-colored car, too? There must be a deep-seated psychological reason for this aberrant behavior. Who cares? Beat them in public.

Fat German men in Speedos.

Fat German men at the nude beach without their Speedos.

The producers and judges of American Idol. You know what? American popular music has been on a respirator since the '70s. The saccharine corporate sludge this show excretes should finally kill it. Replace Simon with Dr. Kevorkian and be done with it. I'm going to go put an old Cream album on. Loud.

Guys who wear stocking caps pulled down over their ears. Possibly the most unflattering fashion statement since the "wrinkled look," which made its wearer look like a Sharpei. This one reduces the unconscious fool to a walking caricature of a penis.

Guys who wear stocking caps and the "wrinkled look" at the same time. Walking caricature of a flaccid penis.

The entire corporate headquarters of Ditech.com. Remember when you used to see commercials about butter? Now all you see are obnoxious home loan ads, mostly from these guys trying to get you to mortgage your future so you can afford butter.

The cruel guys who come up with men's hairstyles. Just watch the Oscars and you will see what has been done to us by these evil hair fascists. What's with this "I just woke up" look? Hey, I know! Don't brush your teeth either and complete that "just fell out of bed look" with a good broadside of morning breath. Or the return of the Beatle cut? Excuse me, but the *Beatles* outgrew this one. Or the thing where they brush it all forward into what looks like a bad day for surfing? Or the one where they comb it all to the middle like the Gerber's baby? Yeah, man, *that's* sexy. Just screams virility. Burp me, momma! So maybe I'm missing something, like since when did looking like a total dork become hip, even if you are Brad Pitt? I don't know. But I'm not letting one of these scissor-happy gel-infusing maniacs touch my head, as dated and unfashionable as it may be. But I do understand one thing now: stocking caps.

Puppy

If I were a puppy
I could climb up into your lap
and nuzzle my wet, adventurous nose between your
utopian breasts
and
you wouldn't even hit me.

Hawaii, Island of Ridiculous Running Birds

For some reason, and I'm not a scientist so I have no idea what it is, birds on this island seem more inclined to run than fly.

Now to any of us who have had the recurring dream of running along the ground only to suddenly take flight and escape from whatever was chasing us, looking down on the trees in wonder and waking to utter disappointment that we are in reality still earthbound, this can only be described as stupid. This feeling is compounded by the scattering of flattened birds that decorate our highways, auxiliary roads and even jeep trails.

There are birds and fowl of all types that have seemingly forgotten what makes their kind special and have decided that the best way to escape danger is to run as fast as possible in front of it for miles. Notable among these are the Indian, or Kalij pheasants, the wild turkeys and of course our ever-booming (and ever stupider) chicken population. But the real stand-outs are two birds that should know better: the mynah and the dove.

Mynah birds are generally regarded as intelligent, for birds. For one thing, they can learn to talk. A dog can't even do this. They are also excellent fliers. Yet they seem to forget this when a car approaches, running as fast as they can — between little spastic hops — to reach the safety of the roadside. More often than not they are successful. But since they do this 24 hours a day by the millions, it is common to see little feathered lumps in the road that used to be mynah birds everywhere you go.

Mynah birds can mimic anything. The sound of a squeaky door, a particular voice, a cat meowing or an old car starting up. Maybe if they spent more time mimicking birds that *fly* away from danger they would festoon less asphalt with their corpses. It's just a thought.

If possible, the doves are even worse about this and not nearly as nimble or fast as the mynahs. Not only do they enjoy sitting blissfully in the road and sunning themselves, it is also their favorite spot for courtship and active mating.

The dove's courtship, if you are not familiar with it, consists of the male cooing loudly while bowing over and over and over to the typically disinterested female. Not only is this eerily human, but dangerous since if you're bowing over and over in the middle of the road, you're obviously not keeping an eye out for traffic. Of course once they actually start mating they are beyond oblivious.

Nothing can ruin a day like running over two mating doves, for them and for you. Not only does it completely spoil the mood, there is something about squashing the universal symbol of peace with a Michelin that stays with you. Unless of course you are a right-wing talk show host, in which case it is sheer poetry.

But since the odds are you're *not* Rush Limbaugh, watch out for our ridiculous running birds. They may fly out of your way and then again they may not. Think of it as Nature's gentle reminder to slow down, take it easy and appreciate the beauty around you. Or at least to avoid the karma of symbolically crushing peace into a bloody smudge on the cement. All the OxyContin in Florida can't fix that.

Hello 21ˢᵗ Century!

I admit it. I'm technology-challenged, one of those poor souls that nerds and geeks and other dweebs who love anything that plugs in or has a battery refer to as "twelve o'clock flashers." That's right, all my electronic devices always read 12:00.

Yet I do use technology. I am writing this on a computer, hoping all the while it will not explode or come up with one of those blue screens that mean the earth is going to be hit by an asteroid in five minutes.

I have cable. A microwave. High-speed internet. A nice stereo. Enough CD's to start my own music store. But I have resisted owning a cell phone with a defiance John Paul Jones or Patrick Henry would have admired, although they probably would have leapt at the chance to have text messaging.

The long fight, however, is over. My girlfriend, who knows what's best for me, gave me one.

Now I only have to figure out how to use it.

The one thing I do like about it is that it's very small and fits in my pocket. That is also the thing I hate about it, because I have no excuse for not carrying it around. Being so small, it is also hard to hold with just a shoulder and the side of my head, like a regular phone, which means I only have one hand free to ward off any asteroid my computer use has triggered.

It also has a camera built into it. This is wonderful for people who want to take really bad pictures and show them to you at the bar while you squint at their phone and say, "Oh yeah, that's really nice."

So far all I've done with the camera is take several pictures of my ear and a couple close-ups of my nose. I did not do this on purpose, it's just that I keep accidentally turning on the camera when I answer the phone.

The first day I had it, it did what most gadgets I've had do: it stopped working. I had no idea why and sat down on the curb to try to figure it out. Fortunately, there was some wino lying there who knew what the problem was and showed me that my battery light was flashing. He also explained the little power bars thingy. I took a picture of his nose.

Really, I do appreciate my girlfriend's desire to ease me into the 21st century. And even a Luddite like myself can see the benefits of having a cell phone, even though it doesn't work at my house because the mountain's in the way. All I have to do is walk a hundred yards out my door and stand in the middle of the road, while keeping one eye peeled for asteroids.

But suppose I had car trouble, or was in an accident. I would then have another option besides screaming for help. I could dial for help and then scream. And, she informed me, the police can now trace a cell phone call so if you're injured in a remote location, they can find you.

"Eh, Dwayne, I spock da car. Stay upside down just makai of da highway neah the 105 mile marker. Checking it out."

"Roger, Kimo, right behind you. Still get malasada?"

"Choke."

"Yeah, look like he *make* only little while. Poor buggah."

"Hmm. No moa skid mark. Maybe he wen fall asleep?"

"Nah. He made one call on his cell. Try check his phone. Maybe he was talking to somebody."

"Ho! No wonder he go off da road. Da buggah wen drive and take picture of his nose!"

Horse Relish

My beautiful and intelligent (and miniature) Chinese girlfriend has a remarkable command of English, for someone who grew up speaking only Cantonese. She speaks without a trace of an accent, but there are still a few phrases she doesn't quite have down yet. So I am writing this to be presented to her on the exact moment of my death. I don't want to screw up a good thing.

Remember when we used to go to Thanksgiving dinner at my parents' house? Remember how much you loved the cookies my mother made? Well, they were not *mink's* meat cookies. As far as I know, nobody makes cookies out of minks, and my mother didn't even have a coat made out of them. Nor were they *minx* meat cookies. That would be a more apt, if somewhat crude, description of you. They were *mince*meat cookies. And yes, they were delicious.

At the same time, Mom would often bake a wonderful ham. I remember how much you loved it, and the mashed potatoes and green beans. You always loved *haole* comfort food. But remember that white, spicy sauce you used to dollop on the ham? You know, the one that would clear out your sinuses like a good jolt of wasabi? Well, I hate to tell you this, but it is not called horse *relish*. That would be something you would put on a roasted horse at a very disturbed barbecue. No, this wonderful item is called horse*radish*. A small point, but it makes a world of difference, especially if ordering in a restaurant.

I'm sure there are a few other corrections I could make for you, but since I'm dead I don't want you to remember me as an overly critical jerk. Anyway, you do very well, much better than I would do if I suddenly found myself forced to speak Cantonese. I can hear the Chinese laughing now. All four billion of them.

So I hope this has been of some use and that you will not think I'm being too critical in offering to correct a few English phrases for you. I'm just trying to be helpful.

Oh. One more thing before I forget. The *Minstrel Period* refers to a time during the Renaissance.

The Running Man

If you spend some time in my island home, Hawaii, you will soon discover that we have no lack of weird and wonderful characters here. This is a safe place for them, I guess. Or maybe it's the climate that breeds them. Who knows? They're here anyway.

Some are hidden away in the deep jungles and you will never see them unless you get lost and stumble across them, which isn't always a good idea. But others come out on the street and are harmless, if unusual.

One such person you can't miss if you come to the Kona side is Cape Man. Cape Man is apparently a very intelligent, normal guy, somewhere in his sixties I would say, who wears (obviously) a cape.

But this is not just any old cape. And he has more than one. All are of his own design and making and are cut from gloriously loud material. A peacock would look drab by comparison. But he does not stop there. He has matching shorts for each cape, as well as these legging sort of things that go from just below his knees to his ankles, like topless bellbottoms. He completes this uniform with matching hats of various alarming shapes. He wears no shirt.

While Cape Man is a definite standout, for sheer visibility and unrelenting endurance as a bona fide Kona character, no one could have rivaled The Running Man. For years I watched him jogging mile after mile down the highway in a pair of blue jean cutoffs and clunky shoes. He is well over six feet tall, has absolutely no fat whatsoever on his body and looks remarkably like George Armstrong Custer.

If Custer could have run this well, he might have lasted a bit longer and kept his hair. He certainly had every reason to run. But I am not aware that The Running Man ever had a particular reason. He just enjoyed running. Miles upon miles.

I have spent many hours with The Running Man talking politics, science fiction and women, me with my Jack Daniels and he with his unlikely Cointreau, holed up on a Friday night at the Liar's Bar. He is not insane. Eccentric? You bet. Insane, no. I never asked him why he ran. I figured it was his business.

Unfortunately, however, you will not see The Running Man if you come to Kona. He has not left us, but has upgraded from running shoes to wheels. He is now The Bicycle Man, his days of endless running being apparently over.

You will see him on the same highway he used to run on, only now he's on a very personal bike with a little overloaded trailer behind it. He still looks like George Armstrong Custer escaping from the glory of the Little Big Horn. You can almost imagine a few hundred Sioux warriors chasing him on their painted mustang tenspeeds.

We still talk over our Jack and Cointreau about politics, science fiction and women. I am still convinced he is not insane. But I miss The Running Man.

I hate progress.

THE SMARTEST CAT IN THE UNIVERSE

"My cat is the smartest cat in the *universe*," my friend Kelly gushed.

I didn't want to hurt Kelly's feelings, or the cat's, but I had to ask why she thought her little calico cat was the smartest cat in the universe.

"Because she knows the answer to *everything*. It's just *incredible*."

I looked at the little cat, sitting there licking herself with one hind leg sticking straight up in the air, and found this difficult to imagine.

"Well, I guess she looks pretty smart, but what does she know the answers to?" I asked as tactfully as I could.

"Just *everything*!" Kelly replied. "Go ahead, ask her a question!"

I had to think for a moment, because questioning cats was something new to me. I mean, I have asked my own cats questions, but rhetorically, you know, like "Who's a good girl?", that kind of stuff.

"What's her name?" I asked my proud friend.

"Stinky Girl."

"Okay. Well, let's see," I said. "Um, uh, okay. What did you do last night, Stinky Girl?"

The little cat stopped licking for a second and looked up at me with a questioning look. "*Prowl*," she said.

"See?" Kelly shrieked with delight. "That's *exactly* what she does at night! She prowls around the yard looking for rats and stuff. Good *girl*!"

I could see where this was going, so I figured I'd just play along.

"Okay, Stinky Girl, who was communist ruler of China from 1949 to 1976, the man responsible for the Cultural Revolution?"

"*Mao.*"

"You're so smart, Stinky Girl," Kelly said, shaking her head in wonder. "I didn't know that one."

Geez.

"Uh, Stinky Girl, what is this part of my head just below my hairline and above my eyes called?"

"*Brow,*" Stinky Girl answered and resumed her personal hygiene.

"Let's see. Okay. The wise men brought the baby Jesus gold, frankincense and what?"

"*Myrrh,*" she replied, then went back to licking between her toes.

"And what do you get when you cross a female horse with a male donkey?"

"*Mule,*" she answered after some thought.

Kelly clapped her hands spasmodically.

"Stinky girl, what is the pointy front end of a ship called?"

"*Prow,*" she answered, stretching.

"See? She could be on *Jeopardy!*" my friend raved.

"Yeah, if she could work the buzzer," I answered. Clearly the time had come to bring this poor woman back to reality. The game had gone on long enough. Stinky Girl was getting tired of it and so was I. And mostly I was running out of questions that could be answered by ambiguous cat vocalizations.

"Okay, Stinky Girl. Who is the worst, most corrupt, most moronic president this country has ever had the misfortune to suffer under?"

Stinky Girl, who was lying on her back with her feet up in the air, rolled over on one side and with a very bored cat look responded, "George W. Bush."

You

Every time I see you

I can't think about anything else

but

the next time I see you

I can't remember why

because

I can't think about anything else.

ALL ABOUT BISCUIT

I have a cat named Biscuit who came to my house uninvited and decided to stay. She was a very young, starving, tiny, stumpy-legged tortoise shell with a couple broken teeth who showed up one day looking for something to eat. I tried to chase her away every day, but eventually gave this useless idea up and fed her. Please note that this is not considered wisdom.

Happily, she began to revive, hissed at me less, eventually climbed up in my lap and made biscuits on me (hence the name) and started to put on some weight. Unfortunately the weight was four kittens, which she proudly deposited under my *hale 'au'au* (outdoor shower). I was not thrilled, but then, it's all about Biscuit.

I went to see my vet and asked about getting our newest family member spayed, suggesting that I would wait until she was finished nursing her kittens, since cats can't get pregnant while they're still nursing. He looked at me like I had a squid sticking out of my nose and implied that he gave this idea as much weight as the nine lives thing and the notion about cats being psychic. I got her spayed the next day because, after all, it's all about Biscuit.

As her four offspring began to grow, I started looking for likely homes for them. My neighbor Charlie agreed to take one, a little female that appeared to have a good bit of Siamese in her. He named her Crumb. One down, three to go.

Another friend wanted the little male orange tiger. He got the adventurous, somewhat exotic name of Tango. So far, so good. Only the twin black kittens left.

Then a strange thing happened. I found that I could not give these two up, unless someone was willing to take them as a set. They were inseparable, playing together constantly or sleeping in a fuzzy ball that appeared to be an unlikely two-headed black cat. I couldn't do it, and Biscuit loved them. And after all, it's all about Biscuit. So I kept them.

A thousand dollars later, I had three outdoor cats. Outdoor, because the one inside, Kiko, and her assistant, Miu, a supplemental cat-like creature, would not go for three more animals in the little house and would not agree that it's all about Biscuit.

On the plus side, the rat population has been seriously depleted. No more noisy all-night rat parties in the attic or buffets in the bird feeder. Biscuit taught her children well, though moving the bird feeder to a new location might be advisable. And I could do without the severed rat heads under my chair on the lanai, thanks. But then, it's all about Biscuit.

And I learned something I should have known all along. When you pick out an animal for a pet, you may or may not get a good one. But when an animal picks *you* out, you are getting something special. Biscuit is a wonderful, loving little thing — if fat, clumsy and a bit homely. Her kids are elegant, sleek and sweet. She knew she would get a good home with us, for her and for her babies, and didn't give up on the idea until she made it happen. Maybe she is psychic, or at least knows a sucker when she sees one.

And when I come home at night after a hard day and sit on the lanai in my old wicker chair, Biscuit stumbles up into my lap, lies on her back and kneads the air while smiling a homely little gap-toothed smile up at me. It makes me very happy she picked me. Suddenly, it *is* all about Biscuit.

Hawaii Dos and Don'ts

Since I live here in Hawaii and deal with that wonderful fact every single day, I figure I know what I'm talking about and that it might be a good idea to give some of you potential visitors a few tips on dealing with our culture.

Hawaii is not like Cleveland, though I'm sure Cleveland has its own list of dos and don'ts, such as: do not bark like a Lhasa Apso at a Browns game; bark like a *Rottweiler* or we'll throw beer on you. That sort of thing.

It's very different here. People will just hit you.

But to make your visit memorable, in a good way, here's a short list of dos and don'ts that will make your stay more enjoyable for all of us.

Do say aloha. It is not corny. Just don't say it like the tour directors (ah-loooooooooooo-HAH).

Don't try to speak pidgin to locals. You will look really *haole*. *Haole* is the Hawaiian word for a white person. Though on rare occasions it can be a term of endearment, it is usually not, especially if preceded by a seven letter word denoting procreation. This is usually how you will hear it. Try not to make that happen.

Do let other cars in and out of traffic. This is a Big Island custom we really love and one that would go a long ways towards making the entire country more livable, if we could export it. If you are in too much of a hurry to let someone else turn into a parking lot, you are in too much of a hurry.

Don't honk your horn in traffic unless you're in a wedding procession (we have the noisiest ones on earth) or waving at someone. You're not on West 57th. This is considered *very* rude. Turn on the radio and practice patience. I hear it's a virtue.

Do take your shoes off when entering someone's home. This is a little custom started by our Japanese Hawaiians. It also encourages good foot hygiene.

Don't walk up to a big local guy and ask him if he's a *real* Hawaiian. He may be Samoan. Enough said.

Do learn to like poi. Okay, at least *try* it. You ate library paste when you were a kid, right? Same thing.

Don't point at a mongoose and say, "Oh, look, Marvin! What a funny squirrel!" This is a dead giveaway that you don't live here.

Do wear aloha shirts. The louder the better. There is no such thing as bad taste when selecting one, although I always wear my more subdued ones to funerals.

Don't get a matching dress to wear with his shirt or vice versa. You may as well tattoo TOURIST across your forehead.

Do enjoy our beautiful ocean. Just remember to *never* turn your back on it. *Swept Away* makes a much better movie title than epitaph. Treat it as you would a vast, wet, inviting Jeffrey Dahmer.

Don't swim at sunset. This is euphemistically referred to as "feeding time." See Don't Pet the Sharks for more on this subject.

Do show respect for Hawaiian culture and especially the sacred sites. While most sacred sites, notably *heiau* (temples) are piles of rocks in various states of preservation, they are still important to the Hawaiians. That means don't climb on them, write your name on them or for God's sake take a stone as a souvenir. By the way, unless you are a Hawaiian, leave the sacrifices to them. Desperate to please the Hawaiian gods? Go pick up beer cans or something, but don't play *kahuna*. This is their *religion*.

Don't scream when you see a gecko. They're everywhere, but harmless. Some people consider them good luck. I consider them extremely messy and have had absolutely no success training mine to use their litter boxes.

Do hang some beads or a lei on the rear view mirror of your rent-a-car. This will help you find it when there are eleven others just like it in the parking lot and you've had six or seven mai tais.

Don't sleep on deserted beaches. While our crime rate is really low, and even though you're on vacation, common sense should still be considered a carry-on. Besides, there are other tourists here.

Do smile and use the shaka sign. Good vibes still go a long way here.

Don't dip your toe in the lava to see if it's really hot. It really is.

Do slow down to Hawaiian speed. Life moves on Big Island, just very, very slowly. People also live longer here than in any other state. There may be a connection.

Don't stare at a Samoan. This will also add years to one's life.

Do try to remember that *we* are *not* on vacation. We live here. If you must stop to take a picture of a sunset or a beautiful tree or something, do it from the *side* of the road.

Don't tell us how it's done on the mainland. We know. That's why we live *here*.

THE FRENCH IMPRESSIONISTS

I am terribly disappointed. For some months now there have been ads on TV and in the newspapers about the French Impressionists coming to town. The tickets weren't cheap, but I saved my money so I could go and waited for the big day. We don't get much entertainment here.

I was not really familiar with the names, being an American, but the tour included Monet, Degas, Renoir, Cezanne and some chick named Pissarro. At least I think it's a woman. The first name is Camille so I'm not really sure.

Anyway, I was not sure what to expect, but I like a good impressionist, and since I'd never seen any French ones, I thought it might be educational as well as funny. You can only watch Rich Little do John Wayne so many times. I figured these guys might do Charles DeGaulle or Maurice Chevalier or maybe even Pepe LaPeu. I was excited.

When I got there I was surprised to find myself in sort of a big empty room with pictures on the walls and everyone just standing around drinking wine. I didn't see any chairs. But this being a French show, I figured it was just their way of doing things. So I took a glass of wine and sat on the floor.

"Excuse me," I said to a guy that looked like he might work there, "When do the impressionists come on?"

He must have been a foreigner because he just sort of stared down at me. Maybe he was one of the French impressionists' agents. So I waited around a while and looked at some nice paintings of flowers and ballet dancers, but the show must have been canceled. After a while, since I was the only one still there, I got up off the floor and left.

On the way out I noticed a sign advertising another tour: The Post-Impressionists. I plan to skip that one. I mean, it would have been fun to see impressions of famous French people but I'm not paying good money to watch someone pretend to be a post. *I* could do that.

How To Be Not Rich

There are people on TV that have a plan, and that plan is to make you rich. There are hundreds of them on infomercials and talk shows promising that if you'll only buy their tapes or take their seminars or read their books you too can be a millionaire.

They're a dime a dozen.

I, on the other hand, have devoted my life to being *not* rich and I will tell you how to do it without selling you anything. Okay, that's not exactly true since you're reading this in a book that you bought. But I didn't title this book *How to Be Not Rich* so that doesn't count. And anyway, you may have stolen this book or borrowed it from a friend or found it in the restroom of a bus station.

The first rule of being not rich is to follow your dreams. Don't do this, however, if your dream is to be rich.

For example, my first dream was to be a musician and get paid enough to stay alive by simply playing music for people. This is one of the best ways I can think of to guarantee you will be not rich. And it's easy. All you have to do is learn to play an instrument and determine to stick with it. Before you know it you will be not rich. I've seen this work not just for me but for hundreds — thousands — of others.

While this particular method was working perfectly for me, I felt I could not rely solely on being a musician to be not rich, so I took the rather bold step of enrolling in acting school. Like all financial plans, it is critical to have a backup and to diversify.

As any waiter in L.A. can tell you, this is a time-tested method of assuring you will be not rich. Again, it requires little expense or training, just the will to do it and a love for acting. I was fortunate to be blessed with both, and though my skill improved and I worked daily on my craft, I managed to stay extremely not rich.

Now some would say that this daring, two-pronged approach to being not rich would be more than sufficient to insure success, but I have always held to the proverb that the three-legged stool is sturdier than the two-legged variety. So I took up writing.

Few occupations, other than music and acting, can not deliver the goods more efficiently than writing. It is a near certainty that if you choose this as a profession you will be not rich. For every Clive Cussler making billions and collecting antique cars by writing unbelievable adventure stories with even more unbelievable dialogue, there are a million guys like me who aren't. You can be one of them.

And unlike Mr. Cussler, you will not be up nights fretting over the screen treatment of your latest novel or arguing with hyper producers with peptic ulcers or dickering about the price on that 1929 Auburn Boattail Speedster over your speaker phone. In fact, you will be fortunate to have a car. Or a phone. But that's the beauty of this plan. And Mr. Cussler will never have the well-defined calf muscles you will surely have from riding that used ten-speed or walking wherever you go.

Your dream of being not rich can come true. I did it. You can do it, too. All you need is the desire and the courage to aim high.

DIMPLE

I caught her

solitary dimple

in my left hand

and let it fly into my homemade rainbow machine

watching

it breathe out smiles the colors of koi and party hats

I'm working on the patent.

The Purple Tunnel

It's gone now, but I remember it. The Purple Tunnel. I used to stand at its entrance feeling more like a spelunker than a hitchhiker. I can still smell the Jacaranda. It still smells like purple. Purple is that smell.

The Purple Tunnel stretched along the top part of Napo'opo'o Road. On those days when the sun determined to change tan *haole* skin to blistered lobster-red, and the tar road seared even lava-hardened feet, it was cool. It may have saved my life more than once. Thank you.

When the Purple Tunnel was blooming, it was more purple than not. The branches were laden with purple, and what they could no longer hold they dropped onto the grateful gray road. Purple above, purple beneath. Cars driving through this scented subway raised a billow of purple that lingered after they disappeared out the other end. Those on foot were splashed with this fragrant purple wave, immersed in purple, drowned in its soft bouquet. Lucky.

The Purple Tunnel is gone now. The ancient trees, their rugged trunks the legs of silent, stalking purple giants, banished like childhood fantasies. Progress doesn't approve of fantasy, however real.

The Purple Tunnel is gone, but I have a picture of it. I took it over thirty years ago with a camera I bought for a quarter. An old Kodak Bullet camera. I hid the picture somewhere. One day I'll find it and be surprised at how purple it really was.

An Adventure of Thorin B Doggo

Many years ago, when I was a kid living on the old McCoy Plantation (before it became a subdivision and was still a hippy paradise), I adopted a small pup. He was given the grand name of Thorin B Doggo.

Thorin was a mutt, a poi dog, or a "plantation mutation" as we called them back then, but a good little guy. He loved avocados and especially bananas (hence the "B" in his name). He went body surfing with me at Napo'opo'o Beach every day. There was even a picture of the two of us doing so in a book about Hawaii. I think it's out of print now. That may have been my fifteen minutes. His, anyway.

Thorin B Doggo was a strange looking little dog, but had a wonderful disposition. He was small, with short legs and a long body and wore a constantly delighted grin. But what made him stand out from the other dogs in the jungle were his enormous ears. They were simply huge, like wings on an airplane, except that they were covered with long blond fur. He was, in short, a chick magnet.

I said he loved avocados. He actually craved them, and when he heard one fall out in the jungle, we had to race him for it. This proved to be his downfall.

One night, we had a particularly nasty storm blow in. The thunder and lightning, rare in Hawaii, echoed through the valley and lit up the jungle every few seconds. The wind screeched and threatened to remove our rusty tin roof. We piled more rocks on it. The rain came from every direction.

Now storms are not much to get excited about when you live in a regular house in a regular neighborhood. But when you live in an old shack without walls perched precariously on the side of a mountain trail, you tend to notice them more. The sound of heavy rain on a tin roof is deafening. It's like living inside Buddy Rich's snare drum. And the absence of walls makes the inside as wet as the outside.

Thorin had gone out to hunt avocados just before the storm hit, and the unusual thunder and lightning must have terrified him. He had never experienced it before. He was lost somewhere in the jungle. The storm continued furiously, bending all the trees back towards the mountain.

Suddenly, through the thunder and the wind and the rain hammering the roof I heard a pitiful, frightened yelp. Then another. It was Thorin's yelp and it was coming from far down below.

I had no flashlight, but I ran from the house barefooted and began to feel my way down the trail, following the yelps as best I could, waiting for the flashes of lightning to get my bearings. There was another yelp, coming from my right. I left the trail and began to work my way down the mountainside, grabbing branches and stumbling over boulders. The yelping grew closer as the rain pelted my face and stung my eyes. More than once I slid and fell, getting scraped and muddied as I worked my way closer to Thorin's panicked cries for help.

A huge crack of thunder exploded above me and lightning illuminated the entire mountain. There below me was Thorin B Doggo.

He seemed to be doing a very strange dance, standing on his hind legs and bobbing up and down with his huge ears sticking straight up in the air like two furry exclamation points. I waited for the lightning, because without it, I was virtually blind and I could only feel my way down to him.

Crrrrack! Now I could see enough to realize he had fallen down a little shelf of lava rock. I carefully made my way down.

Thorin was not exactly dancing. He had fallen off the little cliff in the dark and his enormous ears had been caught, just before he hit the ground, in some of the very sticky vines that grow all over the jungle. His back feet, moving furiously, could not touch the ground. He looked like a terrified marionette.

I eventually managed to work his big ears loose from the vines, and other than being wet and scared, he was fine. I carried him back up the mountain to the relative comfort of my shack as the storm continued to blast the mountainside.

It was during this thankful return trip that I unluckily stuck my bare foot down a puka in the lava rock, ripping the top of my foot to the bone. But as this is Thorin's adventure, enough said.

I gave him an avocado.

Too Much TV

I like TV, especially the old shows that play on TV Land, which are the video equivalents of comfort food, like Mom's meatloaf for the soul. I used to watch news endlessly, until I realized I was seeing the same depressing stories and propaganda over and over. It wasn't making me particularly happy — or informed. Now I get my news from the internet and save my viewing time for fun things or interesting documentaries. But too much TV is not a good thing. Here are some warning signs that might mean you're watching too much:

When you dream, there's a crawl beneath it.

You have carpal tunnel syndrome from the remote.

You insert commercials during conversations.

You have two TiVos.

Your sex life is based around when your favorite shows are on.

You have a TV in the bathroom.

You are trying to figure out a way to fast forward through your girlfriend's lengthy narration of her day at work.

You keep asking yourself, "What would Lucy do?"

You do what Lucy would do.

You are still angry with your father for not being Andy Griffith. And you're sixty years old.

Your car does not run, but you are buying a 60 inch plasma screen.

You can't get all those TV theme songs out of your head. Thirty of them.

You know the answer to every TV-related question on Jeopardy, but can't find Canada on a map.

Your couch has a perfect, permanent indentation of your butt.

Your dog's exercise is watching other dogs on Animal Planet.

You're still fuming over the injustice of the 1989 Emmys.

You think Martin Sheen is actually the president.

You go to church on Channel 27.

You believe that reality TV is just that.

You believe all morgues, forensic labs and police stations are lit like trendy uptown nightclubs.

You speak Klingonese.

You have experienced catatonia during an hour-long power outage.

You have contemplated suicide during a two-hour power outage.

You just bought a generator.

Okee Finds His Purr

When Okee was very new, he lost his mother and his brothers and sisters and found himself all alone in the green jungle and rocky coffee lands, a little orange kitten hunting for bugs and mice and a warm, dry place to sleep. He learned to keep alert for stray dogs that would eat him and bigger tomcats that would beat him up. He was lucky as far as the dogs went, but still got more than his share of whippings from the big cats that moved silently through the trees in the black Kona night.

As he grew to adulthood, this hardship made him lean and tough. But Okee knew something was missing: his purr. Other cats had one, but not him. He looked all over the jungle, in deep brambles, in the tops of the trees and under the shacks that dot the mountainside, but it was nowhere to be found.

"Maybe my mother never gave me one," he said sadly to himself, as he curled up in some soft leaves under a fallen tree for the night.

The next day, Okee went further up the mountain, where he found a small, tumble-down green shack that he had never seen before. He approached it cautiously, because he could smell other cats close by. Then he saw them. There were several, and one black male was particularly big and fierce looking. But he also smelled something else: cat food. If he was clever enough, and quiet, he might get some of this food, which was a lot tastier than rat. It would be worth the risk.

"And," he thought, "my purr might be in that shack."

Well, Okee was indeed clever enough and more. He got the food, but also found that the humans that lived in the shack were kind-hearted and even gave him his *own bowl* to eat it out of. The other cats proved to be tolerant enough, although the big fierce one liked to fight and kept him on his toes. But there was no sign of his purr.

As time went on, Okee settled in and the other cats came to accept him. He would lie on the deck in the sun with them, basking after a good breakfast, and when the human came out and petted them, all the other cats would purr. He would try to do the same, but all that came out was a sort of huffing and puffing noise and a wheezy sound. He was embarrassed and tried to tell the human that he had lost his purr, or that maybe his mother had forgotten to give him one, but the human didn't seem to speak very good cat.

And so it went. The nice human would feed the cats and pet them and all the cats would roll on their backs or rub on his legs and purr and purr. Okee felt very left out, and the other cats started to make fun of him.

"He doesn't know *how* to purr. He's just dumb," the older female snickered to the fierce black tom.

"I think his mother didn't give him a purr because he was too funny looking," he said.

"And I heard that a big ol' rat stole his purr and chased him up a tree," the tiny jellicle female whispered with a giggle.

Okee walked slowly to the edge of the deck and lay down with his back to the other cats. They were right. He *was* funny looking, and without a purr, not much of a cat. He was considering leaving this nice home and going to look for his mother when he found himself being suddenly lifted into the air.

The human carried Okee in his arms and sat down in the big wicker chair. Okee wasn't used to being held, but decided to allow it, seeing how he was already as miserable as he'd ever been.

The human was talking to him, and saying things that sounded soothing, whatever they meant. Okee tried a little cat again, but the human didn't seem to understand and just kept on petting him.

Then the human did something he had not done before. He reached under Okee's jaw and began to gently scratch his chin. The other cats sat up and looked in disbelief at Okee. He was purring. Even Okee was surprised. His eyes widened then slowly turned to yellow slits. He purred louder and louder and began to knead the human's leg.

Okee had found his purr. It was right under his nose all along.

No News Saturday

Like most small towns in America, my rural Hawaiian village has its own daily newspaper. And like most small towns in America, mine has very little going on that would earn an eager local reporter a Pulitzer Prize were he or she to bother to write about it. See, a headline like *"Corruption Discovered in Small Town Government"* would be about as newsworthy (or surprising) as "Scientists discover that men enjoy looking at naked women."

But that's not to say that no one writes about it. They do. We yawn and think about naked women. At least us men do. I can only imagine where the female readers' minds wander to. Probably best not to know.

Aside from petty corruption and good old nepotism, there are also vivid articles on land use disputes, council meetings, banana problems, festivals, local sports and the occasional crime. Of course the banana articles will be read with the most interest because more people have bananas than crime. I tend to think of this as a plus and a concept we should consider exporting. In fact some local reporter, tired of writing about orchid festivals or zoning battles, might want to examine the relationship between the number of bananas per capita and the crime rate. Obviously I was completely wrong in my opening paragraph. I smell Pulitzer.

Our local paper is what a mainlander might think is a bit on the thin side. The whole Sunday edition, even with all the supplements, is about the size of a big city paper's entertainment section. Our entertainment section is smaller than most big city obituary pages. This could be put down to the lack of bananas in big cities or the fact that they have more people ready to die.

Actually we do have several pages of nightlife. It comes out every Sunday. It's called the TV listings.

You may be asking, "What does any of this have to do with *No News Saturday?*" This is a weird thing to do because I can't hear you. But in case anyone was listening to you talking to yourself, I will tell you this: we have no Saturday paper. That's right. Nothing happens on Saturday. And if by some strange chance it did, we could read all about it on Sunday.

You get used to it. Really. Every once in a while I'll slide into the Liar's Bar, pull up a stool and over a Jack rocks ask my friends what happened today.

"I don't know. It's Saturday," they'll say.

"Right," I'll answer.

"Hey, I've got some bananas in the truck if you want some."

Considering that reading the paper rarely fills one with joy anyway, I consider this a pretty good system. I like living in a place that has made *no news is good news* not just a cliché, but a lifestyle, if only for one day a week.

LEAVES

Examining
the leaves on this old sleepy tree
I find a worrisome resemblance
to my own brown scarred hands
Both have profound embossed veins
like mountain ranges and rivers on a globe
skin that has healed and small indifferent hairs
that may or may not have a purpose
This tree, this mango tree, is old
older than me and probably
wiser though what
it knows
what
it's seen
it will
keep
to itself
until
someday
it falls down and
tells the earth all about it.

ALOHA, MID-LIFE CRISIS

I just noticed the other day that I am old. It sorta snuck up on me. I am learning to live with it.

This is not easy. Or fun. But there's only one way to stop getting older, and it's not pleasant. So I deal with it.

I will not buy a Corvette. I will not date teenagers. But I will try to stay relevant. Easier said than done.

Fortunately, I have all my hair. And my teeth. Everything still works. I can cut my own food. I can still wear jeans that I've had forever. But I can't read the small print. Not that I ever did anyway. But now it bothers me.

People in their twenties — even their thirties — humiliate me with respect. Girls see me as a Father Figure. I miss the exciting days of complete disrespect and utter lust. Polite Hawaiian girls call me "Uncle."

I will try to keep going, but I have learned not to play at being young by trying to talk like a kid. I know kids. They know phonies. Trying to spice up my speech with their expressions won't work, because by the time I figure out how to use them, they'll already be passé. I'd sound like a *Dragnet* script. May as well be wearing tie-dye and bellbottoms.

There is one small comfort. All my friends are in the same boat. Even more comforting, in a *schadenfreude* sort of way, is that some of them are not navigating quite as well. Thank God there is always someone to look down on. And make fun of.

Of course, as I get even older, I expect life will become even more challenging. Most likely I will become more opinionated than I already am, and more cantankerous, which is a word only associated with Old People. I may even end up as a curmudgeon. I will be the old weird guy at the end of the bar that the waitresses tease and flirt with, but don't take home. I will piss people off. Intentionally, and not worry about getting the crap beat out of me. I will bore young people to near-death with my lengthy off-topic reminiscences. I will intimidate them with obscure literary and musical references. I will irritate them with my eclectic jukebox choices and play ten old Stevie Ray songs at a time. They will hate me. Good. Screw 'em.

But they'll miss me when I'm gone. I'm going to steal the key to the men's room.

AND WHAT ABOUT MY TOES?

They seem to be all but forgotten, my toes. It's like they're not really that important, just strangely curved and callused afterthoughts. But to my feet, they are ten dusty little soldiers, all deserving of special commendations for bravery and selflessness in the face of extreme danger and brutal hardship.

When you live on an island made of lava rock, and you go barefoot or wear slippers, these ten little guys are bound to see a lot of action. They're my elite scout troops, alerting me to danger continuously by allowing themselves to be brutalized and bloodied, saving me further bodily harm.

Yet do we award them the honor they truly deserve?

Take fingers. At least four of them have names. There's the Thumb, The Index Finger, The Ring Finger and The Pinky. The long one in the middle, which is called The Middle Finger, doesn't really have a permanent name, but The Middle Finger is better than nothing. And in some instances it can be called The Bird. So at least it has a nickname.

Not so with toes. Sure, there is the Little Piggy thing, but this is rarely used once you get old enough to put your own shoes on. I would hardly ever go to the doctor and tell him that I broke The Little Piggy That Had None. But what do you call it? No one knows.

If they were respected, and duly named like fingers, I'd say "Hey Doc, I think I broke my Ring Toe. Again." But there is no such thing as a Ring,

Index or Pinky toe. Worse, the middle toe can't even be referred to as The Bird some of the time.

Okay, for the sake of fairness I should admit that the thumb of the foot is often called The Big Toe. In England they call it The Great Toe. But this is not due to it being held in high esteem but simply because the British have a perverted version of English in which "great" means "big." Still, Big Toe is not really a name, but an obvious and unimaginative description, and the rest of the toes don't even get this.

Someone should deal with this issue and come up with serviceable names for the toes. Maybe William Safire could take up this worthy assignment since he's not that busy right now. Or Buckley. Somebody. But no Latin, Buckley, okay? Keep it simple — simple but meaningful — alright? It's important, because without The Little Piggy Who Went To Market and the The Little Piggy Who Stayed Home I couldn't even wear my slippers.

Big Island, Gateway to Danger

Long before Steve McGarrett wrapped up a case by calmly ordering "Book 'em Dano," another unbeatable detective was prowling Honolulu's mean streets and ridding Oahu of bad guys. His name was Charlie Chan, played by a white guy with tape on his eyes (although they did give him a real *Pake* son). And let's not forget Robert Conrad and Troy Donahue mixing it up with crooks and Connie Francis in the aloha shirt and tiki torch version of *77 Sunset Strip* in the hip (for the 60's) *Hawaiian Eye*.

One would suppose, or at least hope, that these legendary Hawaiian crime fighters would sort of inspire our local cops to apply themselves. This does not seem to be happening, at least not on the Big Island where I live.

Basically, the cops here seem to have only two functions: giving traffic tickets or busting you for DUI. Thankfully, they do not appear to be overly interested in either of these pastimes. This might be because they are especially kind. It might be because they are just a bit lazy. Or it might be that if they really did their jobs, most of the island would be in jail for driving over the legal alcohol limit with a burned out tail light and expired inspection sticker.

In fairness to the local cops, we do have a pretty low crime rate, so they really don't get to practice too much on the real thing. Oh, we have husbands *and* wives (there's some tough girls here) who beat the crap out of each other, the burglaries and shoplifting and even the odd murder now and then, but to a cop from a big city the daily beat here would seem like a paid vacation.

Actually, the cops here are decent enough men and women. On the few occasions I have been forced to call for their services, they have responded immediately. That's "immediately" Kona time, which means in about two or three hours. And again, in fairness, these were not life and death emergencies they were responding to. One was a naked guy running around in the street and the other was kids vandalizing my office (while I was in it). I have no doubt that if I screamed into the phone "Help! I'm being murdered! Help!" they would have gotten here faster. I think. Maybe.

The problem of dealing with any of the real crime here is probably not the fault of the cops, but is inherent in the place itself. For example, yesterday while leaving Kealakekua to get a haircut, I heard a local news bulletin on the radio. It warned that a young man had been robbed at knife-point in a grocery store parking lot in town. The thief had brazenly demanded money and taken the victim's wallet. The newsman then cautioned us to be on the lookout for the criminal and gave this helpful description: a 5'10" local man weighing 200 lbs.

Being a good citizen, I kept my eyes peeled as I drove from Kealakekua down to the north end of Ali'i Drive.

I saw him 274 times.

Anti-Zealotry Solutions

Some of us are pathetically starved for company, but few so famished that a weekend encounter with religious zealots determined to convert one to their particularly narrow dogma is eagerly anticipated. Even here in rural Hawaii — and in my case way up a one-lane road on a mountainside — these determined missionaries will find you on a Saturday or Sunday morning when you're having casual sex or eating chips and watching the game, or all three. This can be a serious fun-stopper.

These people are not easily got rid of. They believe they are doing something mighty important, and a simple "No, thanks" is rarely going to send them back to their bicycles or minivans. Tougher measures are required. For that reason, and to avoid a future intervention and de-programming, I have compiled a list of actions and responses guaranteed to send these humorless proselytizers scurrying for the nearest Kingdom Hall or temple while at the same time insuring they will never return.

1. Answer the door naked. Yes, it's an obvious one, but it really does work. Remember to smile broadly and beg them to come in.

2. Quickly put on a pair of black slacks, a white shirt and a tie. Open the door and say, "Oh, hello brothers. I was just going out to do some missionary work. Gotta run."

3. Say, "I would *love* to talk. Let me ask Lord Satan if you can come in."

4. Say "There's three things I have always sworn to avoid: setting my hair on fire, sticking an ice pick in my eye and joining a crazy religious cult."

5. Tell them you are interested *only* if they practice human sacrifice. You should be holding a large butcher knife and wearing a blood-splattered apron if possible.

6. Eat their tracts and magazines while saying "Mmmmmmmm."

7. Ask them if they allow gay polygamy, because you would hate to have to change your lifestyle.

8. Invite them in and immediately launch into a sales pitch for Amway.

9. Say "Hi. My name is Legion."

10. Say nothing while calmly and quietly setting their tracts on fire.

11. Tell them you're allergic to Kool-Aid.

12. Fill your mouth with pea soup just before answering the door. Do the obvious.

13. Insist that you met one of the two at a gay bar and shared a wonderful weekend in Aruba. Be furious that he dumped you.

14. Demand they kneel at once and worship the true Messiah: you.

15. Ask them for money. A hundred bucks is a good starting place.

16. Answer every question in tongues.

17. Become catatonic.

18. Ask them to please remove their shoes and pants.

CHECK YOUR BOMB

I'm not what you'd call a big fan of flying, so I do it as seldom as possible. I know, I know, it's statistically safer than driving a car to the grocery store, but somehow I find little comfort in that. It's that extra 30,000 foot drop that bothers me.

As a result of being an infrequent flyer, I have been amazed at the new security at our airports. Here at my little Kona-Keahole Airport, they now check in the car and even *under* it when you park. I pulled up a few months ago at the parking entrance and was stopped by two serious-looking security guards. They asked me to open up the back of my car. It's a little SUV (hey, I live on a damn mountain, okay?), so it has a tailgate and I was afraid everything would fall out because it's sort of overstuffed with junk. My girlfriend thinks it's a purse with wheels.

"Okay," I said. "But let me do it." I opened the back.

"What's in that cooler?" one of the guards asked me sternly with suspicion in his narrowing eyes.

"Nothing," I said, opening it and proving my honesty.

At that moment my girlfriend's Chinese sword and several other kung fu weapons of limited destruction clattered to the concrete.

"Okay." They said. As I quickly stowed these lethal objects back in the car. "Go ahead."

The inside of the airport was just as alarming as the outside. The place was swarming with troops in full battle gear. I had only seen this in Third World countries before. Theoretically, these soldiers were there to make me feel safe, but they did not have that effect on me. I found myself wondering if they were all mentally stable, and what if they weren't? I know what a couple hours in an airport does to me, and these guys were already pissed off for getting this lousy, stupid duty — and on a good surfing day — and they were armed to the teeth. I tried to appear harmless. I don't recall smiling so much for so long in my life. I can only thank God I didn't have the urge to wear a *kaffiyeh* that day.

We finally got around to lining up to "emplane" as they call it these days. While standing in line waiting to be strip- and cavity- searched, I noticed a sign informing passengers as to what was *not* allowed on the plane. To make this easy for non-English speaking people, which was just about everybody in line (tour group from Japan), the sign had helpful little pictures. It struck me that most of these forbidden items should be pretty much common sense no no's, even to foreigners, but the last item stood out as an example of taking the ridiculously obvious to extremes of severe mental illness, or of being an idea from John Ashcroft. There, simply drawn, was a picture of a bomb, just like the ones you used to see in *Spy vs. Spy*, black and round with a sputtering fuse sticking out of it. It was surrounded by one of those red circles with a slash through it.

Now I'm looking at this and wondering if they seriously imagine someone is going to be in line and suddenly realize, "Oops! I forgot to leave my *bomb* at home!" and frantically dash off to the men's room and flush it down the john. Or maybe they think this will deter a very stupid (and obedient) would-be terrorist from getting on the plane with a lit cartoon explosive device. All I know is it made me wish I had a black balloon. But it's just as well I didn't. Those guys with the camouflage and M16s would probably not have seen the humor in it. Come to think of it, I can't remember them smiling back at me even once.

When I finally made it to the metal detector, I beeped (of course). I removed everything from my pockets and took off my belt. I still beeped. And because I was not aware that I needed to take off my sneakers, I was pulled out of line and taken to a small pavilion to be further searched. In plain view of all the other passengers, who were by now asking not to be seated next to me, the guard instructed me to undo my pants. I asked him, an enormous black guy that towered over me, if he was kidding. He wasn't.

I undid my pants and folded them down a bit, thankful I had underwear on. He passed the wand between my legs. I beeped again. Not being a member of Spinal Tap I could not imagine what I had in my pants that could be setting off the alarm.

The big, serious guard now warned me that he was going to frisk me. He did this with more intimacy than I was expecting.

"Jesus!" I winced.

Then I suddenly remembered what was setting off the alarm. I had on a pair of pants that unzipped at the knees to convert to shorts, thereby making life much easier. It was the metal zippers. Damn.

When the big guy manhandling me realized this, he did manage a slight smile and said it was okay for me to get on the plane. I thanked him, but added that the next time he wanted to do something like that with me he had better buy me dinner first.

He did not appear to see the humor in that and I did not wait around to see if he eventually got it. I got on the plane and was happily relieved to find an old friend from my local bar sitting next to the last empty seat. He waved and called to me from the rear of the plane.

"Hey, Kona, good to see you, brah!"

"Hi, Jack!" I shouted back.

Bird Seed

I don't know why I feed these birds every morning

doves

saffron finches

papaya birds

java sparrows

and the noisy, unfriendly cardinal

They don't need me

there's plenty to eat without Costco bird seed

Maybe I just like to watch them enjoy themselves

maybe I like their company

as I drink coffee and work crossword puzzles

on the lanai

They make a mess

But every morning they're waiting

waiting for the light to come on in my bedroom

waiting for the front door to creak open

waiting for the sound of a plastic cup scooping seeds out of a bucket

They get very excited at that sound
and pile up in the tree
chattering
waiting for me to sit back down

They'll be waiting tomorrow
and the next day
and the next

One day I won't come out
the light won't go on in my bedroom
the door won't creak open
the cup won't scoop seeds out of a bucket

They'll be very disappointed
wondering what they did wrong
maybe it was the mess
the chattering

I wonder how long they'll wait
before they look for another early riser
who likes birds
and scoops seeds out of a bucket
with a plastic cup.

Commercial Medicine

You can tell a lot about the state of things by television commercials. From what I'm seeing now, I suggest worrying.

For instance, I don't think it's a very good sign when every other commercial is telling you how to mortgage your home. Quickly. This means people are running out of money. And if they run out of money, they can't buy all the other things being advertised, like shower gels that make guys instant babe magnets. For one thing, you would need a shower to use this product, and since most homeless people don't have showers, babes would be unlikely.

The other half of commercial time is taken up by prescription medicines. There seems to be a new one every week. This upsurge may also be related in some way to the increase in mortgage commercials. Somebody should do a study on this.

This sort of advertising used to be illegal, but no more. Now everyone can be his own diagnostician. All you have to do is watch the commercial and tell your doctor how to treat you. This is a time-saver for you and a real break for your doctor, because it relieves him of the burden of figuring out what the hell is wrong with you and what to do about it. He can now save all that hard-earned knowledge for his new book. On golf.

Now it is certainly kind of the drug companies to let us know about their wonderful products, without the hassle of getting this information from someone like, say, a *doctor*, but it is still a good idea to pay attention to the warnings. These little disclaimers are on every commercial, but sometimes they go by very fast, so while you are thanking God for a new miracle cure for what ails you, remember to listen carefully.

For example, say you suffer from depression. That's a bad thing. There's a drug advertised that will make you "happy." That's a good thing. But if you listen closely at the end of the cute commercial filled with little rock-like creatures of some sort, it warns that possible side effects include insomnia, nausea and sexual dysfunction. Now if you were only mildly depressed before, you're going to be having a really bad day. Of course this doesn't rate as high on the bummer scale as the arthritis medicine that promises you a long-shot at cancer and tuberculosis.

Which is why I'm thankful we now have hard liquor commercials in between the money lending and drugs. And while I hardly think this is coincidental, it is something we can actually use, and has in fact been the antidote to money worries and sickness for centuries.

Hey, you know this shower gel smells great!

I Believe

A man's home is his castle, unless he's married, in which case it is more like the bottom part of the castle with conjugal visits.

I will commit suicide by growing so old that it eventually kills me.

Jack Daniels is not just for breakfast anymore.

The football season is too short, the baseball season is too long and poker on ESPN is not a substitute for either.

A man who really knows what women want is a transsexual.

The moon landing was real, but we faked Plymouth Rock.

George W. Bush is the greatest president in the history of the planet: Jupiter.

UFO's, Bigfoot and the Loch Ness Monster are real, but Philip J. Klass was actually a very life-like sock puppet, except for the obvious ping-pong ball eyes.

America suffers from a lack of monkeys.

Some people should really work on developing their inferiority complexes.

Laughter is the best medicine, unless you have scurvy and then oranges are the best medicine.

The Supreme Court should not be photographed sitting down, but hanging from the ceiling like bats.

Ronald Reagan was the apex of the Disney Imagineers' animatronics creations. Nancy still needs a little work.

All women need to be told they're beautiful. And after a few drinks, they are.

All human beings are inherently good, until they learn the word "mine."

Cats are smarter than dogs, but don't give a shit if we know it.

When Life hands you lemons, you should take those lemons and bounce them off Life's goddamn head.

We would like children less if they were born in litters, like spaniel puppies.

'Slow and steady wins the race," unless that race is the 40 yard dash.

Abraham Lincoln was right when he said that "government by the people, of the people and for the people shall not perish from the earth," but he didn't say it wouldn't perish from America.

THE TALE OF THE FABULIST'S NOSE

(With a nod to Lewis Carroll and Edward Lear)

In a tavern quite old
there's a tale that is told
when the moon and the sun interpose
and the barkeep will shiver
and in rye tones deliver
the tale of the Fabulist's Nose.

A liar he was
and he did so because
he was morally challenged and knobby
at least in the knees
so he did as he pleased
making lying much more than a hobby.

He regaled us with tales
of the courtship of snails
and the magical hat-eating bird
and we listened because
he was who he was
and we wrote down all that we heard.

He explained that he'd sneeze

if he ever smelled cheese
and his home high up in the treetop.

And his wife was part fish

and she slept in a dish

and he was the first to play bebop.

His head was so big

because of a fig

that had lodged in his ear as a child.

It was never removed

but his life had improved

and his hair wasn't combed, it was styled.

He had spent his last years

overcoming his fears

by being buried alive in a coffin.

And when he got out

he was ready, no doubt

to finish translating Proust into dolphin.

He once won the Derby

on a horse he called Kirby

of course he was much thinner then.

And he sailed to Hong Kong

wearing naught but a thong

but he couldn't remember quite when.

He had traveled to France
to study the dance
but found himself in The Resistance.
And the medals they gave
for his service so brave
were worn at de Gaulle's insistence.

He had been to the moon
in a hot air balloon
but had found the moonmen uncharming.
So he jumped off a crater
landing safe in Decatur,
the fall fine, but the stopping alarming.

He had once had a cat
that had gotten so fat
that it had to be moved in a barrow.
He prescribed her a diet,
"It works great, you should try it!"
eating skink and occasional sparrow.

He had once had two wings
but like most other things
they were stolen when he wasn't looking.
So now he can't fly,
he said, wiping his eye,
and Caesar's had cancelled his booking.

So we listened for years

and we gave him free beers

as he plied us with lie and with fable.

But what caused his demise

was when to our surprise

he announced he was really Clark Gable.

We took him outside

and we told him he lied

to which he snidely replied "I suppose."

He said this with a sneer,

I said "No more free beer!"

In a flash I had cut off his nose.

I have it here in this jar.

It's the pride of the bar.

I can report it has finally stopped smelling.

So please finish your drink.

You were midway, I think,

in a wonderful tale you were telling.

Thank You, Fox News

A few years ago a study was conducted by the Program on International Policy (PIPA) at the University of Maryland and Knowledge Networks to gauge Americans' perceptions on the Iraq war and determine their degree of support for it. An amazing coincidence was found. It seems that those who relied on Fox News for their information were more likely to suffer from misperceptions than those who watched other networks! The polling revealed that 48% incorrectly believed that evidence of links between Iraq and al Qaeda had been proven, 22% that weapons of mass destruction were discovered in Iraq, and 25% swore on stacks of Bibles that world public opinion favored the US going to war with Iraq. In all, 60% of fox viewers held at least one of these three misperceptions.

As you can imagine, support for the war rose dramatically and proportionally according to the degree of misperception. And while I will fight to the death to preserve others' rights to be willfully — and even dangerously — ignorant, too much Fox News might be a bad thing. Here are some warning signs that it could be time to get your news elsewhere:

You firmly believe that Saddam Hussein personally flew one of the planes into the World Trade Center and parachuted out at the last second.

You believe that all the WMD were secretly shipped to Venezuela.

You believe that any country that begins with I-R-A must be bombed into a pre-Stone Age, radioactive pile of rubble, just to be on the safe side.

You believe this will cause the surviving inhabitants to love us.

You believe that Jesus, like democracy, can be delivered from 30,000 feet or in short, fully-automatic bursts.

You know more about missing white women than any of your friends.

You think Brit Hume is handsome.

You consider Fox to be living up to their motto, "Fair and Balanced" by allowing Alan Colmes to audit Hannity's lectures.

You think Alan Colmes is a liberal.

You have named your three children O'Reilly, Hannity and Cavuto. All three are girls.

You believe that the war in Iraq has been a smashing success. You can't wait to watch other people fight the next one.

You believe George W. Bush is a direct descendant of Jesus Christ.

You think that Jesus could learn a thing or two from George.

You would go hunting with Dick Cheney.

You would go hunting and drinking with Dick Cheney.

You believe Helen Thomas is bin Laden's mother.

You don't understand why "Orwellian" is considered a negative term.

You believe Ann Coulter is a voice of Christian compassion and reason and have a poster of her on your bedroom wall, wearing a leather bustier, thigh-high black boots and holding a whip while kicking a kitten.

You wish everyone would quit bullying O'Reilly, especially that Jew Al Franken.

You have removed the words "loofa" and "falafel" from your vocabulary. Okay, they were never really *in* your vocabulary, but if they were you would remove them.

You find the female Fox reporters extremely sexy. Something about whores with gravitas.

You believe Fox News is actually a branch of the United States government. You are right for once.

The Thing in the Jungle

Hawaii is known for many things: beautiful beaches, killer surfing, temperate weather, glorious sunsets, the best coffee, slack key guitar and hula. It is also known, at least among locals, as a place that can really creep the bejeebers out of you. We call that feeling you get when something sends chills up your spine and your flesh retracts "chicken skin." You might call it "goose bumps."

The late Hawaiian writer Glen Grant spent years collecting Hawaiian ghost stories, which were published in several *Chicken Skin Tales* books and also *Obake: Ghost Stories of Hawaii*. These are great reads for those of us who like to curl up with a bit of weirdness at bedtime (yes, I'm still talking about reading). But I have a story to relate that is completely true, free from any exaggeration and absolutely first-hand. I know, because it happened to me.

Many years ago, in the early 70's, I lived with a friend up on McCoy Plantation, an old coffee farm perched on the mountainside overlooking Kealakekua Bay, scene of Captain Cook's gruesome demise and a mystical place if there ever was one. Like the rest of the young hippie types who lived there, we shared an old coffee shack, nestled in the dense jungle of mango, avocado, ancient coffee and creeping vines that covered the three and four story tall trees.

Today I would consider life there one of hardship, as we had no electricity, running water or indoor plumbing, but at the time we called it "adventure." It was also a much less developed area years ago and when night came, it was dark. Really dark. Our only lights came from candles or kerosene lanterns that seemed to make the night even blacker and reflected countless yellow, red and green eyes in the trees and bushes around us. The jungle was silent at night, except for rustlings here and there and the occasional owl or hawk call and the usual unidentifiable noises that were best ignored.

One day, our friend Jeff came from the mainland to visit us. That afternoon, we decided to take him to visit neighbors of ours that lived up the mountain from us and had something none of us had: electricity, which they bootlegged off a pole on the upper road. We had a great time listening to the stereo and drinking cold beer but as it was getting late, we headed for home.

Being young, we never really planned these excursions too well, and so of course did not bring flashlights. As we headed back down the mountain to our shack, a good fifteen-minute walk away (in daylight), the sun set and being a moonless night it became completely dark, especially under the jungle canopy.

But I was used to this and had learned to navigate the trail by feeling it with my bare feet, which were by now quite tough and leathery. It was impossible to see anything, even the proverbial hand in front of the face, so I felt my way along and kept my arms up in front of me to ward off any low branches. My two friends followed behind in single-file, one gripping the tail of my t-shirt. The greatest danger was to lose the trail (I had once been lost for over an hour only a few feet from it, which was alarming) or to step off it and tumble down one of dozens of 15 foot lava outcroppings that lined the path (which would also be alarming, and painful).

The jungle grew very still and quiet and there was an oppressive feeling in the air. Breathing became noticeable, and labored. The further we went in the blind dark, the more anxious I began to feel. But since I had a visitor with me, I kept going and slowly tested the path. After half an hour, we were almost home. I was feeling the familiar terrain. Soon we would reach a barbed-wire fence that ran behind our shack.

I ducked under a few low-hanging branches, brushed a cobweb from my face and felt my chest hit the rusty barbed-wire. My friends came to a sudden halt, bumping into my back. I groped in the darkness until I found the top wire and stretched it upward so I could climb through the fence.

Slowly I slid my right leg through the gap so as not to snag myself on the rusty barbs and placed my foot down. My weight came down on my right foot. But what my bare foot was standing on was not dirt, not lava rock or grass. I was firmly standing on a body. A very large body.

Underneath my bare foot, I felt movement. Slow, writhing, undulating movement as whatever it was began to crawl. There was no sound, just the impression of large, strong muscles and hairless skin slowly rippling beneath me.

Without a word, I pulled my leg back through the fence and led my wondering friends another way around until we reached our shack.

Of course as soon as it was light I went to check the fence out with my friends, who by now knew the details. There was no sign whatever of anything large having been lying on the ground.

I have spent hours trying to imagine who (or what) I could have been standing on. We had large wild pigs and donkeys up there (still do), but neither of these would have reacted that way to being stepped on, and both have hair. Neither would have remained silent.

Again, a person would have said something. Even a drunk hippy passed out on the rocky ground would have at least groaned. And it didn't feel like a person. Not at all. It was unnatural in feel and movement. And huge. There was a coldness to it that I can still feel to this very day.

It gives me chicken skin even now to think about it.

But every once in a while I wonder if somewhere, maybe on the lush mountainside above McCoy Plantation, there is some now older and wistful creature writing, as I am now, about a very strange experience it had years ago in the lonely jungles of Kona when something, who knows what, stepped on it and ran away.

WABI

She doesn't know how beautiful she is. That's the problem. It does no good to tell her. She thinks she's flawed. Maybe she is.

I could tell her about the Japanese artists and their use of the *wabi*, the intentional flaw they will place in a lovingly crafted vase. Their belief is that this sometimes even unnoticeable flaw gives the piece more value, makes it distinct. Unique. One-of-a-kind.

I could tell her all about the concept of *wabi-sabi*, the Japanese aesthetic idea that delights in the beauty of imperfection. A way of viewing the world that sees beauty in the unconventional.

I could tell her this, but she wouldn't listen, even if I were a Japanese artist. But I'm not, so I just tell her that she's beautiful and hope some day she'll see it for herself, flaws and all.

INTELLIGENT DESIGN

Lately a furious debate has been raging between nuclear physicists, paleontologists, chiropractors, televangelists and other men of science as to whether the theory of evolution should be taught in our schools. The dissenters believe some other explanation should be taught, one that has the catchy name "Intelligent Design."

I am not a scientist. I'm a writer, and so have not devoted much time or thought to this subject, spending my days foraging for food and surfing internet porn, but I determined to find out more.

Luckily, my local community college offers a course in their Continuing Education Series based on the Young Earth Theory, an offshoot of Intelligent Design, and so I enrolled in the once-a-week night course.

Reading the synopsis of the class was very interesting. According to the pamphlet, the course will show how humans and animals of all kinds — including dinosaurs — lived at the same time and inhabited the same geographical regions. Examples of human footprints found with dinosaur tracks, among other inexplicable and anachronistic evidence, will be studied. There are to be numerous guest speakers and a short film series to augment the text.

I was excited. Thursday night came and I took my place in the classroom, front row. The professor, an energetic young fellow with an unusually high-pitched voice, gave a short introduction and announced that we would begin with the short film promised in the literature. He dimmed the lights.

The film was a colorful animated work from the 60's and began with a large group of cavemen working a vast rock quarry and demonstrating a level of cooperation I would not have thought them capable of. In addition to this obviously well choreographed labor, they were assisted by various animals — enormous and powerful dinosaurs — that had been harnessed for cartage and even digging, like giant herbivorous earth movers.

Amazingly, considering the time period and level of development, these primitive men had some sort of union, for at a given time, a bird squawked, and all work subsided. The primary character, at this point, slid down the back of the dinosaur he had been operating and jumped in some sort of rudimentary automobile which he propelled with his bare feet.

The home life of these ancient people was no less surprising. On arriving at his shelter, also made of rocks and bearing an uncanny resemblance to a modern ranch-style suburban home, his skin-clad wife met him at the door, as did the family pet, a young and very frisky dinosaur. In the house, the conveniences were much more creative and modern than I would have given these ancestors of ours credit for as well. They had managed, with little but rocks, sticks and the odd animal to construct record players, can openers and vacuum cleaners.

Needless to say, I came away from this first class with a newfound admiration for our primitive progenitors as well as a hearty respect for the Young Earth Theory and Intelligent Design. There is simply no way primitive man could have created automatic dishwashers on their own, even knowing that mastodons could blow water out of their trunks. A Higher Force must have been involved. I only wish Darwin himself could have been at that class. He would have had some very serious explaining to do.

As you can well imagine, I am now hooked on the idea of furthering my education. Next semester promises to be equally exciting and informative, with a course entitled "Living in the Future." It is supplemented by another film, this one about a family that lives in a sort of space tower, drives flying cars, pushes lots of buttons and has a female robot maid.

If I had known science was this much fun, I wouldn't have slept through my physics class in high school.

Bodysurfing with Mark Twain

I go bodysurfing with Mark Twain,

his happy ghost with fluorescent *haole* skin

mainland feet

and draggled mustache above a wry smile

that says I was truly happy

here

and nowhere else.

Ever.

Mark Twain loved Hawaii.

He became Mark Twain here

trading in Sam Clemens for good

sitting by the pier in old Kailua town

watching the complaining cattle cow-paddle to the boats

with *paniolo* wearing red-checkered shirts

on swimming horses

beside them

hollering in Hawaiian.

Sam Clemens invented Mark Twain

while eating dried *opelu* and drinking *okole hao*

here

and nowhere else.

Ever.

I go bodysurfing with Mark Twain.

We wait for a good wave,

bobbing in the water and humming

until he says, "Now!"

We both swim for it like lifeguards

rescuing drowning girls

beautiful drowning girls

only to miss it at the last second

and end up laughing and spitting out ocean

here

and nowhere else.

Ever.

Mark Twain never saw Hawaii again.

He never saw the monkey pod tree he planted in Na'alehu

with his own ink-stained hands

grow so tall

or drank too much with leathery cowboys

or laughed at their long-winded lies

or slept with a brown Hawaiian girl

with smooth warm skin

and long ginger-scented hair

on a cool still night

again

or lazed in the shade on a hot afternoon

in his shirt sleeves

smoking a cigar under a coconut palm

and remembering her.

He was happy

here

and nowhere else.

Ever.

So I go bodysurfing with Mark Twain.

THE TOWN THAT EATS CARS

Who built the Great Pyramid of Egypt and how was it accomplished? What happened to famed aviator Amelia Earhart? What really crashed at Roswell, New Mexico in July, 1947? Why does my nose look bigger from the right than from the left? These great, unsolved mysteries of our time continue to puzzle us, but there may be none more mystifying than the enigma of Kainaliu, The Town That Eats Cars.

Kainaliu squats like a quaint speed bump between Honalo and Kealakekua on the west side of the Big Island, Hawaii, and actually is a village, not a town, but The Village That Eats Cars doesn't sound quite as creepy.

Kainaliu straddles the Mamalahoa Highway, a two-lane road, complete with charming Polynesian potholes, that circles the island, and the part of the town you can actually see is comprised of a few boutiques, Oshima's Drugs, a gas station, the old Aloha Theater, a massage center and a coffee shop with incredibly crass signage. It is here that the mystery unfolds daily.

I say "daily," but actually the bizarre activity only occurs on weekdays, during rush hour traffic (yes, we have rush hour traffic).

As anyone knows who leaves Kailua or points north after work and heads south, traffic will come to a near standstill after passing Keauhou, and one will inch forward for miles until reaching Kainaliu, The Town That Eats Cars.

Valiant attempts have been made to solve this unearthly puzzle and correct the traffic situation to boot. For example, our Council, in their near Buddha-like wisdom, have decreed that no cars may park diagonally at Oshima's during the late afternoon hours, because the backing-out process impedes the flow of traffic. Orange traffic cones stand in haughty defiance of those who would ignore this dictum. Of course this means all the drunk carpenters must parallel park their trucks when they stop to get more Steinies. The verdict is still out as to whether this is helpful (or sane).

Not satisfied with the results of this alone, our leaders have by fiat ruled that no cars may enter the clogged Mamalahoa Highway from the Old Highway above after 3:00 pm. This is intended to keep the traffic moving and (reasonably) force those who would use this route to butt in line to politely wait their turns. This strict edict is enforced by granite-jawed uniformed officers and a daunting, if flimsy, white wooden barricade.

Yet the problem persists, as does the eerie mystery. For as one creeps forward, around the curve by Teshima's Japanese Restaurant and down towards Kainaliu, The Town That Eats Cars, a feeling of horror grows, and one can sense the hairs on the back of one's neck rising and the cold, clamminess of chicken-skin spreading from head to toe. For as sure as it's raining right now in Hilo on someone's wedding, the traffic will miraculously vanish as soon as one passes through Kainaliu, The Town That Eats Cars.

Where did it go? Where are all the cars that were bumper to bumper only minutes before? Were they mere phantoms? Mechanized night marchers? No one knows.

Have they been spirited to an alternate reality? Another dimension? And how, one will ask oneself, did I make it through alive to tell the tale? For the road ahead is now clear with only a few cars in the hopefully safe distance. Yet a cautious, fevered glance in one's rearview mirror (should one muster the force of will to look) will reveal the endless traffic still mutely, but relentlessly following, still inching forward in fitful starts and stops, still crawling inexorably towards the Unknown and the inescapable date with destiny in Kainaliu, The Town That Eats Cars.

The Deadliest Arts

My miniature girlfriend is a martial arts master, having devoted herself for years to honing her skills and reflexes and teaching others how to defend themselves as well as unite mind and body into a harmonious, serene, Zen-like killing machine that can pull your heart out and show it to you before you die.

This means I don't mess with her.

Not that I can't take care of myself, but when someone can simply touch you with a finger and send you to the floor in howling agony, it's best to talk things out. Or just say "yes." This makes life simpler and less painful.

Of course she is not the sort to initiate any conflict and has never even hinted at pulling my heart out, but I figure it's best not to give her a reason to consider it.

Being a kung fu master, my miniature girlfriend has taken this arcane knowledge and physical prowess and directed it towards everyday life, creating in the process several disciplines of her own, all distinctly and brutally feminine. In these she remains unrivaled and unconquerable.

Probably her most impressive style is the urban form Sha Ping, which is generally used in crowded environments in which the martial artist must deal with more than one adversary at a time. An offshoot of this, Shu Sha Ping, is even deadlier and more focused. The heel strike in this form is lethal.

Only a fool, or one with suicidal tendencies, would interfere with a female master engaged in these forms. Successfully overcoming either Sha Ping or Shu Sha Ping will inevitably lead to defending oneself against the hideously clever and ruthless Wai Ning form, to which there is no defense but shame-faced, ear-plugging retreat.

After many years of living in the presence of these possible perils, I have learned to avoid conflict entirely and seek peace and harmony at all times. For if one manages to overcome these deadly forms, there is still the most frightening and horrible of all that she can fall back on, that which no man wishes to face: the silent, grim and debilitating Nun Fo Yu, a discipline so menacing, so cruel that it makes Shu Sha Ping seem like an evening in a hot tub with a snifter of brandy and twin Amish farm girls.

As the victim of this most frightening form on several agonizing occasions over the years, I have learned what to do and more importantly what not to do. In the words of Sun Tzu, author of *The Art of War*, send flowers and pray.

CATHARSIS

When poetry tumbles

out of your head

onto

the page

it's not writing

it's purging

without the mess

THE WORLD SERIES

Right now I am enjoying the World Series. It's actually only just started, with the Red Sox up two games to none over the Cards. I am guessing the Sox will win, but that's not the same as betting money on it. I really don't care either way. I live in Hawaii, not Boston or St. Louis. There will be no riots in Kealakekua regardless of which team wins or loses. But we can watch the mayhem on TV and it will be just like being there, except the weather will be better.

Normally I don't watch baseball. I find this sport a bit less exciting than The Weather Channel. And weathermen are less disgusting since they hardly ever spit tobacco juice while scratching their crotches.

Baseball could be exciting, but there would have to be some rule changes. I would allow tackling. Exploding baseballs would make it more watchable as well, especially if the balls were timed to go off at odd intervals.

"It's a full count...runners on the corners...and here's the pitch... Martinez swings and..."

BOOOOOOOOM!

It would also give new meaning to dying on third. I'd watch.

What I like most about the World Series is the fact that it proves how geography-challenged we are. America is a big, nice, friendly, slobbering puppy of a country, but it does not make up the whole world. It seems that if we are going to call it The *World* Series, we should maybe allow the rest of the world to play. Sure, countries like Lithuania and Kajikistan probably couldn't field a contender, but Cuba, Japan and the Dominican Republic just might. At least they're good enough that we keep taking their players and putting them on our teams. And the Japanese would be easier to tackle.

Anyway, game three is tonight. I feel duty bound to watch it. It's like voting: it's a pointless and stupid waste of time, but something an American should do.

In the meantime, my girlfriend and I are going to resume our best of seven ping-pong match. She's from Kailua. I'm from Kealakekua. I'm one game away from Galactic Champion.

Winston's Hill

Winston's father bought him a small hill in the Valley of Low Expectations. On this hill he built his house, and a little chapel for hurling conditional prayers at a sleeping God.

Winston lived alone, dreaming.

The small brown people of the valley envied Winston's house and chapel and took time from their daily labors to stand at the border of his land and gaze up the small hill at his two splendid buildings.

"If we work very hard and save our money, someday we too may have houses and chapels on small hills," they would say.

So they did. The small brown people toiled and sweated and saved their pennies in jars buried deep in the dark, wet earth of the valley, marked with stones. They sent their prayers to a distant heaven on the uncertain, pale smoke of cook fires and sighs.

Winston lived alone, dreaming.

The small brown people worked until their fingers were tough and crooked like oak twigs and their backs bent as if always carrying an invisible, crushing burden. Yet they took comfort in their labor. They thought of houses, of chapels, on small hills.

Winston lived alone, dreaming.

Winston dreamed on. But when he woke, he would hobble to his chapel and hurl a prayer heavenward, hoping to wake his God.

"Oh God, please get me out of this valley, out of this house, out of this chapel! Let me till the ground and herd the sheep and bundle the wheat. Release me from this solitude, this small hill, my prison. Let me go."

Winston died alone, dreaming.

The valley became known as The Valley of Buried Pennies. To this day, visitors come to see the one small house and one small chapel on the one small hill.

Judy's Wings

Judy has six different sets of wings she wears depending on the occasion and her mood.

The first pair she wears only for light housework and dealing with tow truck drivers who have lost all hope.

The second set is for planting roses in freshly tilled beds and kisses on crying babies' heads.

Another is for wishing for the wind and hoping for the rain. It involves a dance, a cup of sweet tea and the image of a white, running horse.

Yet another is used only at midnight when the last embers fade out and the cat sits alert staring at the ceiling. These are danger wings, made of obsidian and the webs of orb spiders.

The fifth set is for perching atop cathedrals and hailing invisible cabs splashing and swerving down cobblestone streets.

The last set, yet to be used, are to enfold her in slumber when all things are safe, all things are done, everything is in its place and the world creaks to a halt on its axis with a sigh of relief.

Kona Lowell still hides out on the Big Island, Hawaii, way up in the mist with his miniature wife, Chee, an assortment of odd cats and one rather small, supplemental cat-like creature named Miu. He is also the author of *The Solid Green Birthday & Other Fables*, to which this is the long overdue follow-up. A musician and composer as well, Kona is the leader of the progressive rock band, No Empty Sky, whose first CD, *Empire*, contains the only progressive rock song ever written about Hawaii, *Yellowbird (Hawaii Nei)* and is not nearly as silly as the rest of the stuff he does.